National Library of Australia Cataloguing-in-Publication entry:
Amphlett, Rachel – author

Look Closer

ISBN: 978-0-9922685-4-1 (paperback)
Amphlett, Rachel, author
Look Closer
A823.4

Look Closer

Rachel Amphlett

Chapter 1

London, April

Will Fletcher rested his head against the door pillar of the taxi and let the washed-out cityscape pass by the window as he wiped tears from his eyes, trying to calm his adrenalin-spiked heartbeat.

The taxi driver was doing his best not to stare at him in the rear-view mirror but failing spectacularly. Instead, he steered the vehicle around back streets and one way systems in an attempt to get his passenger to the hospital as fast as possible.

Will sniffled.

After their argument last night, he and Amy hadn't spoken this morning. Instead, she'd left before he'd had a chance to apologise, and now he wished he hadn't been so stupid.

He reached over and pulled his backpack across the seat towards him, patting the outer pocket to make sure he still had Amy's mobile. She'd forgotten it in her haste to leave the apartment before he could speak to her, and in an attempt to make peace, he'd been planning to phone her and hand it over during their lunch breaks, maybe buy her dinner after work.

He pushed the bag away, his hands shaking.

He'd been out when he heard about the accident. He and Russell Harper had escaped the confines of their offices at the museum in search of a caffeine fix. He'd been running late as usual, his flight from his desk interrupted by his manager.

Twisting his back to ease the cricks in his muscles, he'd turned to see Jack watching him from his office.

The older man had raised an eyebrow. 'If you're getting coffee, you'd better buy me one,' he growled.

'White, no sugar – 'cause you're sweet enough already, right?'

Jack had held up his middle finger in Will's direction and turned back to his room, closing the door.

Will had laughed and made his way down to the lobby. As the elevator doors opened, the cacophony of hundreds of languages had assaulted his ears.

Tourists swarmed around the entranceway into the museum, pointing out exhibits to each other, calling out to wayward children as harassed tour guides led their charges through the building, hand-held signs wavering above people's heads.

Will had nodded to a uniformed security guard as he passed through one of the exit turnstiles, and then hurried across to the front doors where Russell was waiting for him, tapping the face of his watch.

'You'd be late for your own funeral,' he'd grumbled, then grabbed Will's arm and propelled him through the doors.

'Remind me to get a coffee for Jack,' said Will. 'Otherwise you'll be top of that invitation list.'

'And how is the old bugger?'

'About normal for a Monday.'

'That good, eh?'

'Uh-huh.'

They had followed the wrought iron boundary fence that encircled the museum and then turned left, passing Georgian houses on a tree-lined avenue.

Stationary cars parked into impossibly small spaces lined each side of the street, while the road itself flanked the side of the museum's grounds before veering right.

'What's Amy working on these days?'

Will shrugged. 'This and that,' he said. 'It's all very hush-hush – she wouldn't even give me any details.'

Russell had laughed and slapped him on the shoulder. 'It's okay – I won't ask. Guess we'll just have to both read about it on the front page, huh?'

Will had checked over his shoulder for traffic before both men hurried through a small park, jogged across a zebra crossing and into an Italian restaurant. The aroma of freshly ground coffee beans teased his senses as the door swung shut behind him.

'Good morning, gentlemen!' A beaming man, black hair speckled with grey and silver streaks, appeared at a doorway. He'd checked over his shoulder into a noisy kitchen before wiping his hands on a tea towel slung over his shoulder and moved towards the coffee machine. 'Usual?'

'Please, Luigi.' Will had turned at a light punch on his arm. 'Oh yeah, and one for Jack. Better make it a double shot – given the mood he's in, I don't think his funding came through.'

Luigi made apologetic noises and busied himself with the coffee-making machine. 'It's not good, Will. I have seen all the hard work he puts into those exhibitions.'

'Well, maybe we'll hear something this week,' Will said, then turned and joined Russell, who had pulled out two stools next to a counter set against the window overlooking the street. For a moment, he had sat and watched people as they dashed backwards and forwards in front of him, then looked down as Russell grunted.

'What?'

'Just reading this newspaper article. About that prick they reckon will be Prime Minister one day, heaven help us. Did you know he used to work in construction?'

'No.'

Russell had flicked the page, a snort of derision on his lips. 'My old man reckons the guy's a crook – lots of dirty deals, you know?'

Will had grinned, not wishing to be drawn into a debate. He knew if Russell started, the man wouldn't shut up until they'd returned to the museum. He sneaked a glance at the photograph which accompanied the newspaper story and realised it was the same man Amy was meeting with that morning. He checked his watch.

'Here you go.' Luigi had interrupted his thoughts and set three Styrofoam cups on the counter in front of them. He tapped the lid of the one nearest to Will. 'That's Jack's,' he instructed, then winked. 'With double shot.'

Will had slid off the stool, picked up his and Jack's coffees and stepped towards the door. 'Cheers, Luigi. See you tomorrow.'

He had his elbow against the door handle before he realised Russell wasn't behind him. 'Russ?'

His jaw slack, he had turned to see Russell staring at the small television above the bar. Will followed his gaze to see a news bulletin splayed across the screen.

A red *Breaking News* banner screamed a headline across the lower half of the display, its white, bold text jolting Will out of his good mood.

Opposition leader ambushed by gunmen. Several casualties.

'Luigi, turn the sound up!'

Russell took the remote control from the restaurant owner and aimed it at the television, the newscaster's voice bellowing from the speakers. They all jumped at the sudden blast of noise, before Russell adjusted the volume.

The newscaster had his finger to his earpiece, reciting updates as the newsroom relayed them to him.

'We're told that emergency services are at the scene, and the road has been blocked to all traffic while police deal with this serious incident,' he said excitedly, then dropped his hand and returned to the autocue in front of him. 'For those who may be just tuning in, we're receiving reports that Ian Rossiter, the current favourite to win next month's election, has been involved in an incident in Marylebone. There are reports that he has been shot, alongside the people that were in his car with him.'

Will had squashed the sides of the coffee cups in his hands, his knuckles white. His heartbeat had rushed through his ears, punching him between the ribs, the reporter's urgent voice washing over him.

'Will? Are you okay?'

'I think Amy was with him.'

'What? What do you mean?'

Will had pointed at the television with one of the cups. 'Amy. She told me she was going to interview Ian Rossiter this morning. Some sort of exclusive.' He blinked, fighting down the panic. 'I – I just know something's happened to her.'

Russell had glanced at Luigi, then back at Will. He snatched the coffee cups away, thrust them at the bewildered restaurant owner, and then frog-marched Will through the front door.

'I'll call you later, Luigi,' he'd yelled over his shoulder as the doors slammed shut.

Will had allowed Russell to lead him back to the museum, the passing pedestrians and traffic a blur. Somewhere in his subconscious, he heard car horns, exclamations from people who didn't get out of Russell's way fast enough, a vehicle skidding to a stop to their right, and a man's voice swearing from an open car window.

Then they were at the security turnstiles. Will had felt like he was walking underwater. He could hear people, but he struggled to understand what they were saying. Russell leaned across in front of him, reached down, and tugged at the security pass clipped to his belt. Ignoring the curious glance from the guard, Will had pushed through the gate, and then Russell's palm shoved him in the back, pushing him towards the elevators.

Will's hearing only returned to normal once the doors slid shut. 'Sorry – pardon?'

'Oh thank god, he's back to earth,' muttered Russell. 'I said, we'll make some calls. Her mobile phone might be out of range – or flat, right?'

'No – she forgot her phone this morning. It's in my backpack.'

'Where's yours?'

'On my desk.'

'Well, phone her editor – find out if she's back at the office.' Russell slapped him on the arm as the elevator doors opened. 'Come on buddy, hang in there.'

Will's composure had started to slip as Jack barrelled through the open-plan office towards them, heads turning to stare as he approached.

'You need to get to Prince George Hospital as soon as possible,' he blurted out. 'We've been trying to call you for the past twenty minutes.'

Will had frowned and noticed the man's eyes were red-rimmed. 'Prince George Hospital?'

'It's all over the news – someone's attacked Ian Rossiter and everyone in his motorcade,' said Jack and lowered his voice. 'Amy's been shot.'

Will had felt his legs buckle, and Jack reached out to steady him. Sweat broke out on his forehead and blood rushed in his ears, blocking out the conversation.

'Have you got enough money on you for a taxi?' his boss asked. He looked over his shoulder. 'Rosalind! Get a taxi ordered for Will. Have them pick him up outside the loading bay round the back, okay?'

Will watched, helpless, as the young intern had launched herself at her phone, speed-dialling the local taxi number, her eyes wide, staring at him. Somehow in the last thirty seconds he'd become rooted to the spot.

Then Russell was at his side, thrusting his backpack at him. 'Go, Will. I've put your mobile in there. Get going. Phone us when you can, all right?' He nodded at Jack, and then pushed Will towards the elevators. As they waited for the doors to open, he'd lowered his voice.

'Jesus, Will, of all the people for this to happen to. I mean, god – I hope she'll be okay. If there's anything I can do, you'll let me know, right?'

Will had raised his head at the sound of a low *ping* as the doors opened. He stepped inside the elevator car, then turned to face his friend, tears at the corner of his eyes, and nodded.

'Yeah, of course.'

Now, he was stuck in traffic and still two miles away from the hospital.

When he'd wondered why Amy hadn't been taken to one closer to the scene of the shooting, a remnant of information in his subconscious reminded him that the newly opened Prince George complex boasted one of the best neurosurgery teams in the country.

He rubbed his hand over his face and tried to ignore the sickness in the pit of his stomach, and then the taxi lurched forwards once more, and they were moving.

Please let her be okay.

Chapter 2

Will rubbed his eyes and tried to ignore the pervading aromas of disinfectant, sweat, and fear that permeated the corridor. He shifted on the chair, its metal back support cool against his shirt.

He felt a bead of sweat pool between his shoulder blades and pushed back into the chair to stop it from running down his spine, then leaned forward and put his head in his hands, his mind racing.

What the hell happened?

Last night, as they'd sat at the small dining table in the apartment, their plates pushed to one side, Amy had asked him to collect her laptop from their computer expert on his way home from work the next day.

'Has he finished the upgrade?'

'Yes, said it was good to go. Faster processor, the works. Shame I haven't got it for the morning – I'll have to hot-desk when I get into work to type up my interview.'

'Did you pick up spare batteries for your voice recorder?'

'Yeah.'

She'd collected the plates together and walked the few paces into the open plan kitchen. After shoving the dirty dishes in the sink of hot water, she'd returned to the dining table.

'So, when are you going to tell me who you're interviewing in the morning?'

She'd sat down and pinched the stem of her wine glass between her fingers. 'I wasn't planning on telling you until afterwards.' Her eyes met his. 'I know what you can be like.'

'What do you mean?'

She'd exhaled and leaned back in her chair, before taking a sip of her wine.

'Stop stalling, and tell me.'

Amy had put the glass down, and then told him.

'Ian Rossiter? Are you out of your mind?' Will had pushed back his chair and paced the living area. 'What were you thinking?'

'It's the story of my life, Will. This could be such a career boost for me.'

He'd spun around, his hands on his hips. 'And what has Kirby said about this?'

'I guess he reckons it's time I got a break,' she'd said. 'After all, I've been there two years. I've proved myself to him. And,' she said, as Will had snatched his own wine glass from the table, 'it was my idea.'

'You're crazy.'

'And you're just pissed off I'm doing this my way, not yours.'

He'd stormed off then, slammed the door to the bedroom to lie in the darkness, alone, fuming, eventually falling asleep.

When he'd woken up, Amy had already left for work.

Will raised his head at the sound of footsteps. A man in his late fifties with a shock of white hair hurried towards him.

'Will Fletcher?'

'Yes?'

'I'm Mr Hathaway – the surgeon who will be operating on Amy.' Hathaway shifted his grip on a clipboard and extended his hand. 'Let's talk in the privacy of my office.'

'Isn't she in surgery? Why aren't you there?'

'They're prepping her now. As you can appreciate, it's a very delicate balancing act, so we need to be careful.'

Hathaway led Will down the corridor, then abruptly turned left, pushed open a door and ushered Will inside. He pulled out a chair for Will at a paper-littered desk, and then sat.

'Are there any relatives nearby we can contact to be with you?'

Will shook his head. 'No.'

The surgeon nodded. 'All right.' He flipped over the pages on the clipboard, and appeared to be lost in thought.

Will's foot tapped against the worn carpet, until he could bear the silence no more. He leaned forward.

'How bad is she?'

Hathaway sighed. 'The bullet is lodged in the outer part of her skull. It's going to be a long procedure – hours – with a very specialised team. After that, we'll be keeping her in an induced coma to give her body time to heal.'

'What happened to Rossiter?'

'I'm sorry, Will. Patient confidentiality...' The surgeon leaned forward. 'I'll need you to sign the paperwork,' he said, pushing the clipboard towards Will and lifting the pages until a consent form became visible. He pulled out a black soft tip pen from his overcoat and passed it to Will.

As he leaned over the desk, the pen slipped from Will's grip and rolled across the desk.

The surgeon stopped its movement with a slap of his hand, and then glanced up. 'I promise I'll do my best, Will, but I won't know how bad it is until I start.'

Will nodded, took the pen from Hathaway, forced his hand to stop shaking, and scrawled his signature across the bottom of the form.

'You're not going to want to hear this,' said Hathaway, 'but go home and wait for me to call you. It'd be better than sitting in one of the waiting areas here – that's not going to do you any good.'

Will closed his eyes. 'Can I see her now?' His voice shook, and he felt tears pricking his eyelids. 'Would that be possible?'

'She's in a very sterile environment while we're prepping for surgery, but you can see her through a window.'

Will nodded, opened his eyes, sniffled, and then looked at Hathaway. 'Just do everything you can for her, okay?' he croaked.

The older man nodded. 'We will. Come on.'

He stood and led Will through a network of corridors until they were side by side at a window, its curtains closed. Hathaway peered between a crack in the material, then partially opened them.

Will put his hand over his mouth.

Amy lay on a hospital gurney, swathed in blue sheets, her fair hair shaved on one side, her left cheek purple and bruised, congealed blood covering her face. Tubes and machines surrounded her while nurses worked, inserting needles, checking displays on screens and quietly talking, sharing information.

He groaned. She looked so helpless, so utterly vulnerable, and there wasn't a damn thing he could do about it.

He jumped as Hathaway gently put a hand on his shoulder. 'She's not in pain. She's medicated at the moment.'

Will nodded, unable to speak.

Hathaway turned to look down the corridor. 'The police will probably want to talk to you in a bit.' He lowered his voice. 'They're going to put an armed guard outside the operating area and on the room we'll put Amy in for her recovery.'

Will's brow creased. 'Armed guard? Why?'

Hathaway shrugged and let the curtain fall back into place, and gestured towards the waiting area. 'I don't know. They haven't told me. Sorry, Will – I have to get ready for her surgery.' He pointed towards a row of chairs placed under a television set, its volume a low hum under the noise of the ward. 'You can wait here for the police. They've set up a room elsewhere in the hospital. I'll phone you as soon as I'm out of surgery to let you know how it went.'

Will nodded dumbly, shook the surgeon's hand, and traipsed towards the row of chairs. As he sat facing the television placed on the opposite wall, the twenty-four hour news channel replayed the footage he and Russell had seen earlier that morning.

The reporter's conjecture became increasingly excitable as he reiterated the scant facts the news channel been able to glean from the police and various experts in counter-terrorism.

Will pushed the palms of his hands down on to his thighs to stop them from shaking. The man's retelling of the events seemed oddly cold, with little humanity entering the man's voice as he described the situation as if it were mere entertainment.

'Mr Fletcher?'

He jerked his head in the direction of the female voice.

A young female police officer stood at the end of the row of chairs, a look of genuine concern on her face.

'Yes?'

'Please come with me, sir. The detective in charge of the investigation would be grateful if you could speak with him now.'

Will followed the policewoman as she led the way to an elevator. At the third floor, she waited until Will joined her in the corridor, and then led him through a series of offices and into a conference room. Knocking twice, she opened the door, stood to one side, and gestured to Will.

'Inspector Lake, this is Will Fletcher.'

Chapter 3

Detective Chief Inspector Trevor Lake stood, extended his hand to Will and indicated that he should take the seat opposite him.

The desk had been cleared, along with the rest of the room, for the detective's use.

'Thanks for your time, Will,' he began. 'I can appreciate this must be very difficult for you at the moment.'

Will nodded, mumbled a thanks, and sat down, dropping his backpack onto the floor next to him.

Lake sat facing Will and turned to a clean page in a small notebook. 'I'm just going to ask a few questions, to get a feel for what Amy's movements were this morning.'

'Okay.'

'Did she say where she was going?'

Will shuffled in his seat. 'She was really excited,' he began, and then coughed to clear his throat, realising his voice had started to choke. 'She'd landed an interview which could have been the career break she'd been after since we left university.'

Lake nodded. 'Did she tell you who the interview was with?'

Will nodded. 'Yes. Ian Rossiter.'

The detective paused to scribble some notes into the notebook.

Will remained silent, transfixed by the detective's scrawl across the page and wondered how the words would be translated back at the police station. He noted Lake's accent, tried to figure out where he'd come from, and settled on Wiltshire. Something about the softened consonants. He wondered idly how the detective had ended up joining the Met, and then frowned.

'Why is there an armed guard outside the operating room?'

The detective's head shot up. 'Who told you that?'

Will shrugged. 'I saw two of them walking towards the room when I was talking to Amy's surgeon,' he said, and then wondered why he'd so easily lied.

'It's just a precaution, due to the nature of her injuries and how she sustained them.'

'You mean because she was shot when she was with Ian Rossiter.'

'Exactly.' Lake lowered his gaze and returned to his notebook. 'Did Amy say where she was meeting Rossiter this morning?'

Will frowned. 'No, she didn't, actually. I'd assumed it was at the newspaper offices. It seems wrong that a politician would willingly walk into a newspaper office, though.'

Lake smiled. 'Indeed it would. No, they met at the Three Birches Hotel in Marylebone. According to the staff, Amy had arranged to have a breakfast meeting with Rossiter.'

'That would make sense. She said she was going to go into the office and type up the interview now I think of it.'

The detective nodded, wrote something on the notepad. 'Did you or Amy have a fight this morning?'

'What are you trying to imply?'

'It's okay, calm down. Standard question I have to ask.'

'Well, we didn't.'

'Did Amy seem on edge lately, perhaps stressed?'

Will leaned back in the chair and sighed. 'No more than usual. I mean, her job is really busy, and if she's chasing a story, I'll often find her asleep at the kitchen table where she's been working all night to meet a deadline,' he said, 'but she thrives on it – especially the last couple of weeks. I've never seen her so excited about a story.'

'Do you know what the angle of her story is?'

Will shook his head. 'No, I don't ask, because usually, she can't tell me anyway. I only found out last night that she was going to interview Rossiter.' He leaned forward in his chair, put his elbows on his knees, and dropped his head into his hands. 'I can't believe this is happening.'

'Hang in there, Will, you're doing well,' said Lake. 'Just a few more questions, and we'll be done here.'

'It appears that your girlfriend, Amy, and Ian Rossiter met as planned for a breakfast meeting at the

Three Birches Hotel at nine o'clock. The hotel staff we've interviewed told us that at some point during that meeting, the conversation got a little heated – raised voices, a brief argument – before Rossiter stood to leave. Amy appears to have managed to placate him, and they finished their breakfast, although the same hotel staff also told me that it appeared a short-term truce had been struck, because the tone of the conversation afterwards was noticeably strained.'

'Do you know what they discussed at the hotel?'

'No. Amy's notebook and voice recorder were taken from her at the scene of the incident by her attackers.'

'Why would they do that?'

'We don't know yet. That's one of the avenues of investigation we're pursuing.'

Will swallowed. 'What happened between the hotel and the place where everyone was shot?'

Lake leaned forward and folded his arms on the table. 'I'll only tell you this, because the press is going to have it figured out soon anyway. Around ten thirty, Amy and Rossiter left the hotel. Amy paid the breakfast bill, and then followed Rossiter to a waiting car outside the hotel. Rossiter's bodyguard took the front passenger seat.' He paused. 'We'd naturally assumed that Rossiter offered to drop Amy off at her workplace – it was still raining hard.'

'What went wrong?'

The detective shifted in his seat. 'For some reason, the driver decided to take a short cut, rather than a direct route to her offices. As he drove along that street, a van cut in front of the car, two men with guns jumped out from the back, and attacked the occupants of the car.'

Will paled. 'Go on.'

'The driver was shot first – to prevent him from trying to manoeuvre the car out of the way. Then the bodyguard, then Amy.'

Will frowned. 'Why shoot Amy?'

'We don't know, Will – we don't know who we're dealing with yet, and we're still conducting interviews. Maybe because she was a witness.'

'Where did they go – the people that shot her?'

'Unfortunately, it seems they picked the location of the attack at a point they knew they'd be sheltered from CCTV coverage,' said the detective. 'They were professionals, but we've got people scouring all the cameras in the vicinity right now, as well as the local underground stations.'

'What happens next?' asked Will, lifting his gaze to look directly at the detective. 'What are you doing to find the people who shot her?'

Lake sighed, tossed his pen on to the desk, and leaned back into his chair. 'I'm sorry, Will. I can't discuss that – it's still an open investigation.'

Will peered at his fingernails. The one on his right thumb was bleeding. He didn't even remember biting it down to the quick. 'What about Rossiter? Why didn't they kill him?'

Lake leaned back in his chair. 'We don't know.' He ran a hand through thinning hair. 'We think they heard the sirens and panicked – lucky for Rossiter, as he only sustained a flesh wound to his shoulder.'

'Shame they didn't panic sooner.'

The detective ignored the remark. 'My officers are still collating witness statements. I shouldn't even be discussing this with you,' he said. 'I'm just hoping you might remember something which will give us a lead, a reason why this has happened.'

Lake reached into his shirt pocket and pulled out a business card. He slid it across the desk towards

Will. 'I think I've got enough for now, but please, if you remember anything Amy's told you in passing or find anything that might help us catch the people that did this to her, phone me immediately. It doesn't matter what time of day or night.'

'What happens if you don't find them? I mean, after Amy recovers – what happens then? Will she always be in danger? Will they come after her?'

The detective shrugged, an apologetic expression on his face. 'I'm sorry, but I can't answer that. Not yet. But we will make sure she's safe while she's here.'

Will stood up, shouldered his backpack, and slipped the detective's card into his trouser pocket. 'Then I guess we're done here.'

'Thanks again, Will,' said Lake. He stood and opened the door. The smells and sounds of the hospital echoed along the corridor outside. 'I'll let you know as soon as I can tell you anything.'

'That's all I seem to be hearing this morning,' said Will.

Chapter 4

Will stood on the pavement outside the hospital, his mind numb.

Beside him, a toddler chattered away excitedly to her mother who sat on a bench under the bus shelter, half listening to her child while she sent texts and checked messages on her mobile phone, a cigarette hanging from her lips.

Behind the bus shelter, the Accident and Emergency department of the hospital remained busy, its doors opening and closing as regularly as clockwork, ambulances delivering a steady stream of casualties from the busy weekday city. Voices wafted across the breeze to where Will swayed with his thoughts, broken only by the sound of the bus as it braked to a halt, the doors hissing open.

Will stood to the side, letting the mother and toddler onto the bus before him, and then made his way to the empty rear of the vehicle. He slid onto a seat nearest a window, pulled his backpack onto his lap and rested his head against the glass pane as the bus pulled away into a steady stream of traffic.

He wanted to cry, the tears already forming, his throat raw and ready to let it all out. He beat his fist to a tuneless rhythm on the rubber seal of the window, the scenery passing in a blur.

He rocked as the bus came to an abrupt stop, and then smeared condensation off the glass with the sleeve of his jacket and watched as the bus made its way through the city.

Forty minutes later, Will climbed off the bus and began walking home. He jumped as his mobile phone began to ring, and reached into his pocket, his fingers brushing the detective's business card.

'Hello?'

'Will, it's Jack. How are you? Any news?'

'Not yet – she's only just gone into the operating room,' said Will. He could picture his boss pacing his office as he spoke, his dark grey hair pushed this way and that by his hands as he fought with bureaucracy for funding for his beloved archives department.

'Well,' said Jack, interrupting his thoughts, 'take as much time as you need to be with her, Will. Your job will be here waiting for you.' His voice was brusque, no-nonsense.

Will's lips pursed. He heard Jack struggling to keep his composure under the circumstances. His boss had first met Amy at the department's Christmas party two years ago, and with their love of research, the pair had got on well.

'I will, thanks, Jack,' he said, not wishing to prolong the conversation. 'I've got to go.'

He hung up, put the phone back into his pocket, and pushed open the front door to the apartment block. Entering the lobby, he swore as he spied the sign pinned to the elevator doors, and then he altered course and pushed open the heavy fire exit door and began to climb the stairs to the eighth floor.

As he climbed, he began making lists in his head: the friends he'd need to call to stave off any rumours the media may have started about Amy's condition; her editor who would be concerned for her, but already sending her colleagues to report on the new angle to the story; and clothing and toiletries to take back to the hospital which Amy would need while she recovered.

A heavy grinding sound penetrated his thoughts as he reached the sixth floor, and he cursed, and then leaned against the whitewashed concrete wall, sweat running between his shoulder blades.

The elevator was back in working order.

He eased himself away from the wall and slowly walked up the remaining flight of stairs. Reaching the eighth floor, he pushed open the fire exit door and began walking along the corridor towards the apartment. Reaching into his pocket for his keys, he thumbed through them while he walked until he found the small bronze-coloured one for the front door.

He glanced up to insert the key into the lock and froze, his mouth open in disbelief.

The lock had been broken. Splinters of wood protruded from around the brass lock, paint chips from the door frame scattered across the carpet under his feet. The door itself was closed against the frame – anyone casually passing the apartment would not have seen the damage caused.

Will touched the scrape marks around the lock. A chisel or file had been used, the work thorough but not necessarily professional – a rush job.

He looked over his shoulder, back along the corridor, but no one appeared from the closed doors of the fire escape. The elevator sign at the end of the corridor blinked the letter "G" once.

He stilled his breathing and listened. A television played loudly from the apartment two doors along, where an old lady lived, but he could hear nothing from within his home.

He slowly pushed the door open, treading sawdust across the threshold, his heartbeat thudding steadily in his ears.

The sheer devastation to the apartment was evident from the short narrow hallway which led through to the kitchen and living area. Pictures had been pulled from their hooks on the wall and lay broken on the thin carpet, their frames splintered among the shattered glass that crunched under his shoes.

Bile rose in his throat as he entered the living area, his arms limp by his side as he slowly lowered his backpack to the floor, and then carefully walked into the room and circled the damage.

A knife, or the tool used to break the front door lock, had been used to slice through the material of the matching sofa and arm chairs, the stuffing strewn throughout the room while the chairs had been tipped over, the underside linings ripped to shreds. The small coffee table had been turned upside down, scattering magazines and the television remote controls onto the floor. The dining table had been up-ended, the four accompanying chairs fallen onto their sides.

Will raised his eyes to the kitchen area, where cupboard doors had been pulled open and the contents spilled over the tiled floor. Glasses, plates, and coffee mugs had been thrown onto the floor, and Will's feet kicked against cutlery which had been tipped out of drawers onto the tiles. Even the refrigerator had been emptied, the smell of discarded food already beginning to permeate the air, along with a faint trace of cigarette smoke.

Will blinked, recalled the elevator being out of service, then realised he'd nearly walked in on the intruder.

He retched, and quickly crossed the living area to the floor-to-ceiling windows which opened out onto a small balcony. He pulled aside the curtain and yanked open the glass door, then stepped outside and breathed deeply, filling his lungs and fighting the urge to vomit.

As he concentrated on breathing, he glanced down to the street below and the small park opposite the apartment block. Two toddlers screeched with delight as they were pushed back and forth on swings by their mothers, while a commercial airliner banked high in the sky above them as it took off from the city airport. In the distance, a dog barked as a siren passed its gate, and then fell silent.

Will wrapped his fingers around the guard rail and gripped it hard, his knuckles turning white. Everything seemed so normal, so peaceful. He turned and surveyed the inside of the apartment, realising he hadn't even investigated the damage to the bedrooms and bathroom yet, and not really trusting himself to begin to look.

He inhaled deeply, then stepped from the balcony back into the apartment, and picked up each of the dining chairs in turn, before pulling up the table from the floor. He turned to the coffee table, set that upright and crouched down, reaching out and gathering the scattered magazines towards him before placing them on the table.

He stood then, and put his hands in his pockets, at a loss what to do next. His fingers brushed against the detective's business card and his mind jolted. Pulling it from his pocket, he glanced at the number scrawled across the top of the card, then pulled out his mobile. He began dialling the number and then cursed as a message appeared, indicating the battery was nearly flat.

His eyes swept the debris-strewn carpet until he found the battery charger, plugged in the mobile phone then went hunting for the landline phone among the trashed apartment.

In four strides, he cleared the room and found the telephone pulled from the wall socket. Amy had insisted on keeping a landline at the apartment in case of emergencies. He smiled grimly at her prescience.

Will plugged the cable back in, and carried the phone across to the dining table, sat heavily in one of the chairs and put his head in his hands, rubbing at his hair as his mind churned. He breathed out slowly, sat upright and reached out to dial the emergency number.

His backside left the wooden surface of the chair as the phone began to ring while his fingers were only a fraction away from it, his heart surging painfully between his ribs.

His hand shaking, he wrapped his fingers around the receiver and picked it up. 'H-hello?'

The voice at the other end was husky, low and urgent.

'Do you have her laptop?'

Chapter 5

'What?'

Will frowned, part of his brain asking why the police were asking for a laptop computer, the other part screaming at him in warning.

'Do you have the laptop?'

'No.'

Silence filled the line, a faint hiss distorting the empty space.

Will cleared his throat. 'I mean – I don't have it at the moment. I can get it.'

'Good. Good.'

Will frowned, trying to concentrate. The voice was male, older, a little gruff as if the person had once smoked, or still indulged in an occasional nicotine fix.

'Here's what I want you to do.' The man paused. 'Are you listening, Will? This is important.'

'I-I'm here, yes.'

'Good.' Another pause, and this time, Will heard the faint dragging sound of an inhaled cigarette. 'You're going to bring that laptop to me.'

'Who are you?'

'You're not in a position to ask questions, Will. Just do as you're told.'

Will picked up the phone and began pacing next to the table, the adrenalin beginning to surge through his veins, the anger rising. 'Who the fuck are you? Did you break into our apartment?'

'I'm the person who can kill Amy, if I want to.'

Will fell back into a chair, his legs shaking. 'What do you mean?'

'No questions, Will.' Another pause. 'Now, the laptop computer. Does it have a password on it?'

'Yes.'

'And would you happen to know what that password is?'

'Yes.'

'Good.' Another drag on the cigarette. A breath out. 'Now, Will, the really sensible thing to do would be to let me have that password now and leave the computer switched off when you collect it. Are you going to be sensible?'

Will frowned, then turned his head and looked at his backpack.

'I'll know if you tried, Will.'

'What do you want?'

'I want you to put this phone down in a moment. You're going to leave the apartment without calling the police. And you're going to collect the laptop from wherever it is, and then bring it to bus stop number forty-four on Wimbledon Hill Road by three o'clock. Leave it on the seat there and walk away.'

Will glanced at his watch. 'That's only two hours from now!'

'It wasn't a request.' The caller's voice had lowered dangerously, his impatience piercing the line. 'What's the password on the laptop?'

Will recited it, and then held his breath, only the sound of his heartbeat thumping in his eardrums for company for what seemed like an age, and then the caller spoke once more.

'Two hours. Use them well.'

There was a soft click and then the tone of a dead line.

Will lowered the receiver from his ear, glancing at it once before laying it in the cradle. He sat, stunned, for a moment, and then the inertia left him.

Climbing over the debris scattered across the carpet, he scrambled towards his mobile phone, which was now showing a partly-charged battery. He ripped out the power cord and scrolled through the contact list until he found the one he wanted.

Pressing the 'call' button, he waited until, after three rings, the phone was answered with a distracted 'Hello? City Computer Services?'

'Simon, it's Will.'

'Will! My god – was that Amy I heard about on the news this morning?'

Will heard the sound of a radio being turned down, the music fading into the background. 'Yeah, yeah it was,' he murmured. 'Hey, Simon, what exactly did Amy get you to do with that laptop of hers?'

There was a brief pause at the other end of the line. 'Nothing much. I just put more memory in there and added a faster back-up drive. Amy wanted the files she'd saved on it tidied away – said she was going to be working on a big story for a while and didn't want to be distracted by anything else. Why? What's up?'

Will took a slow breath. 'She saved all our insurance details on here somewhere. I was hoping you could copy them for me or something,' he lied. 'With everything going on, I thought I'd better, you know...'

'Sure, sure,' said Simon. 'I understand. If you come over to get it now, I'll sort it out for you straight away.'

Will glanced at his watch. 'Sounds good,' he said. 'I'll be there in about forty minutes.'

'No problem. See you when you get here.'

Will hung up and bit his lower lip. As much as he hated lying to his friend, he knew he didn't have a choice. If he was going to have to hand over the laptop to a complete stranger who was threatening to kill Amy while she was in hospital, he wanted to see what was on her computer.

He slipped his phone back into his pocket, dropping the charger into his backpack. He shouldered the bag and glanced around the trashed apartment once more. He had the fleeting thought that perhaps he should get the police involved, then immediately dismissed it.

The caller's instructions were clear, and if the apartment was being watched, then he'd be putting Amy in even greater danger.

Chapter 6

Will left the apartment and pulled the door shut after scraping the worst of the splintered wood over the threshold with his foot. Until he knew exactly what was going on, he didn't want to draw attention to the mess and have one of the neighbours phone the police in his absence.

He pressed the call button for the elevator, waited for what seemed like an eternity, then gave up, and pushed the door to the fire exit open and ran down the concrete stairs to the street.

He forced himself to walk along the road towards the bus stop, pausing only to glance over his shoulder, wondering if the mystery caller was watching.

As he drew closer to the end of the street, a single decked bus drew away from the stop, belching black diesel fumes from its exhaust as it accelerated into the traffic on the main road. Will cursed, turned left and hurried towards the nearest underground station.

He tried not to push past the elderly couple at the top of the escalator leading down to the platforms and gritted his teeth as they chattered away in front of him, oblivious to his impatience. As soon as he reached the bottom of the stairs, Will brushed past them, tossed a muttered apology over his shoulder, and rushed onto the north-bound platform as a train slid into the station.

As the doors hissed open, he stepped into the cramped carriage and pushed towards the end, then turned and watched the other passengers. Paranoia swept through him as he scanned their faces. Most ignored him or glanced up and caught his stare, frowned, and looked away.

He rubbed the bridge of his nose with his fingers, trying to release the pressure building up into a headache, his body swaying with the motion of the train as it sped along the tracks under the city. A trickle of sweat ran between his shoulder blades, and he shifted the backpack on his shoulder to hide the damp patch forming on his shirt.

He knew the underground line route, but nervously glanced at the map glued to the carriage wall above the windows while the train pushed through the stations, as if he could make it go faster. As his stop drew closer, he pushed his way unapologetically back through the carriage towards the sliding doors and held on to the handle above his head as the train burst out of the tunnel and slid to a halt at the station.

Shoving his body past a trio of slow-moving garishly dressed tourists all talking at the top of their voices, he walked quickly towards the exit and stepped onto the escalator. His fingers tapped impatiently on the rubber handrail as the stairs moved towards street level, and then he burst past the remainder of the pedestrians and slipped through the gate with a practiced flick of his wrist at the ticket barrier.

Hurrying along the street, his throat parched, he stopped at a newsagent to buy a bottle of water, not bothering to wait for the loose change that the Indian man behind the counter waved at him. He tipped half the contents of the bottle down his throat before re-capping it, and then turned up the road towards Simon's computer business.

The sound of approaching sirens failed to seep into his consciousness until he was almost at the street corner.

Will glanced up at the first police car that tore past him, its brake lights flaring as it reached the corner of the street and turned right, before an ambulance and a second police car followed within seconds of each other.

He frowned, picked up his pace and was running by the time he reached the corner and turned into the road on which Simon's shop was based.

Located above a coin-operated laundry and a café, with its front door squashed between the two, Simon's computer business was set up in such a way as to keep a low profile among his neighbours, to avoid drawing attention to the thousands of pounds worth of equipment on the premises.

Will slid to a standstill on the pavement as he rounded the corner, his mouth open, his breath passing his lips in gasps as he stared at the scene in front of him.

A small crowd had gathered to the rear of the two police vehicles that had been parked to create a makeshift cordon either side of the computer shop's front door. Blue lights flashed, reflecting off the windows of the shops on either side.

The front door to Simon's computer business was open, the narrow stairs with their threadbare carpet visible. In front, the ambulance had parked, the back doors open.

A policeman appeared at the bottom of the staircase, his face pale. Will watched as the man glanced at the small crowd, squared his shoulders and strode over to his car, radio to his mouth as he spoke to his control room.

A woman was standing to one side of the entranceway to Simon's business, being comforted by some of the other bystanders.

As Will drew closer, he heard her telling one of the younger policemen that she owned the coin laundry, heard a gunshot and saw the outline of someone leaving Simon's place in a hurry, their features disguised by a hood, before she went upstairs to check on her neighbour.

The rest of the conversation was lost as she burst into tears, and the policeman reached out and put a hand on her arm.

Hitching the backpack up his shoulder, Will approached an old man who stood staring at the commotion with a Jack Russell on a lead which hovered next to the man's ankles. As Will approached, the man glanced over at him, his dog glaring up at the intrusion.

'What happened?'

The old man shrugged. 'Burglary gone wrong by the looks of it.' He nodded towards the coin laundry. 'Woman who owns that says she heard shouting upstairs, then a couple of gunshots.' He shook his head and turned, tugging the small dog after him. 'Don't know what the world's coming to.'

Will watched the old man shuffle away, then checked the street for traffic before crossing and approaching the people milling around outside the café. A woman watched him draw nearer, her hair piled up on her head with a pen stuck through it and a tea-towel slung over her shoulder, two mugs of coffee in her hands.

'Want a coffee, love?' she asked as he stepped onto the pavement next to her.

He shook his head. 'No thanks. How long ago did it happen?'

She shrugged. 'About twenty minutes ago.' She glanced at his backpack. 'Hoping to get your computer fixed, were you?'

'Something like that.'

'Yeah, well, you might want to take it somewhere else,' she said. 'I don't think that place is going to be open for business any more.' She excused herself, walked past him and up to the police car, where the constable relieved her of the two coffee mugs, turned, and walked back towards Simon's shop.

He glanced over his shoulder at Will as he passed, opened his mouth as if to speak, then changed his mind and began to climb the stairs away from the street. He stopped at the third tread, retraced his steps, and then stood to one side.

Will wiped his forehead as the ambulance crew appeared, walking down the stairs, shaking their heads. A man in a creased suit followed behind them, a harried expression clouding his features. Will guessed him to be a plain-clothed police officer.

As the crew turned towards the vehicle, a van braked next to it, its liveried panels confirming Will's fears. He covered his mouth to silence the cry that nearly escaped as the van's occupants climbed out, pulled pale blue all-in-one suits over their clothing, and turned towards the building, their faces grim.

Will reached out with his hand and leaned against the building he stood next to, his head swimming. As he watched, the ambulance crew started the engine and drove the vehicle away, its lights still, its siren silent.

Will turned on his heel and began to put some distance between himself and the row of shops. He hurried across the road, and then turned left, away from the main street. He stopped, out of breath, and leaned forward.

Only a few hours before, his life had been safe, Amy wasn't in the hospital undergoing emergency surgery, and the biggest problem he was faced with was trying to get the attention of the coffee barista in the café down the road from the museum.

He raised his head at the sound of his mobile phone ringing. He pulled it from his pocket, noticed the caller's number had been blocked, and took the call.

'Hello?'

'We've got a problem, Will.' The now-familiar sound of a cigarette being inhaled reverberated down the line.

Will stumbled, regained his balance, and sat on a set of stone steps that led up to a dentist's surgery. The words on the brass plaque above his head blurred, his head swimming as the caller's voice spoke softly into his ear.

'There's nothing on that laptop of your girlfriend's. She and your computer friend thought they were being clever.'

'What did you do to him?' Will whispered. 'What have you done?'

'I'll phone you again in one hour, but keep moving,' said the voice. 'The police are at your apartment, thanks to one of your neighbours. Don't go back there if you want to keep Amy safe.'

The caller fell silent, and the incessant beep of a dead phone filled the space.

Will lowered the phone from his ear, stunned.

He cradled the device in his hand, the sickness crawling through his stomach, sending goose bumps racing down his arms.

He took a couple of deep breaths, then pulled his backpack off his shoulder and tucked his phone inside. His fingers brushed against another phone.

Amy's.

He pulled out her smartphone and frowned when he saw the display showing a missed call, then checked the volume control and found it had been switched to silent.

He glanced at the time stamp on the message. Ten o'clock that morning.

'That doesn't make sense,' he murmured. 'She was interviewing Rossiter then.'

He slid the on-screen lock to the 'off' position and typed in Amy's four-digit password.

The voicemail icon was flashing. One message.

His heart pounding, Will pushed the 'play' icon and then pressed the phone to his ear. His fingers trembled when he heard Amy's voice.

'Will, if you're listening to this, I'm either in danger, or I'm dead. I need you to do something for me. They'll be looking for you.'

Chapter 7

Will closed his eyes, and let Amy's voice wash over him.

'Jesus, Amy,' he whispered. 'What the hell is going on?'

'Will, there's not much time,' Amy's voice continued in a murmur. 'You need to be careful. I don't think you can trust the police, either. I'm not sure.' She broke off, and he heard her flush a toilet. 'I'm hiding in the ladies' at the Three Birches Hotel… Jesus, Will, how could I have been so stupid?'

Will used his sleeve to wipe the tears away from his cheeks, ignored the man who stared at him as he hurried by the steps, and pressed the phone closer to his ear.

'Simon wiped my laptop on Friday afternoon,' said Amy, talking rapidly now. 'I didn't think that once I'd met with Rossiter and given him my ultimatum, something like this might happen. I think he'd already worked out that I'm onto him. We put the contents of my laptop onto two hard drives. You need to go and get those, Will. They're your only protection at the moment.'

'I've put both hard drives in our private mailbox at the Holborn Post Office,' she said. 'Along with some notes and a letter. You have to do what I've written in the letter, Will – it's the only way to stop them.'

She paused, her soft breathing echoing down the line. Will closed his eyes, and imagined her pushing her long fringe away from her face, the way she always did when she was deep in thought.

'Don't trust anyone, Will. People will kill for this information – if you're listening to this, they already have.'

She sighed, and then the message ended, before the phone company's robot voice intoned how to delete the message, how to repeat the message, and how to save it.

Will listened twice more, just to hear her voice again, before he saved the message and switched the phone off to save the battery.

Re-shouldering the backpack, he glanced down the street, and then hurried towards the underground station.

Get the hard drives and the letter, she'd said.

Follow the instructions.

***

Will slowed as he approached the side of the post office, stepped aside to let an old woman through the entryway, and then hurried down the alleyway to the post box he and Amy shared.

He pulled his keys from his pocket, inserted the right one into the lock, and paused. He glanced over his shoulder, his gaze wandering over the other customers as they queued.

Was he being watched?

He fought down the paranoia, and turned back to the small square door of the box. He twisted the key and peered inside.

Sweeping aside that month's gas bill and a marketing brochure from a mobile phone company, he spotted a slim white envelope with Amy's neat handwriting imprinted on the front.

He slid it out of the box and frowned.

Where were the hard drives?

He craned his neck to better see inside the dark crevice and then smiled. Turning his wrist, he pulled the padded envelope that had been taped to the roof of the box. He moved his body to shield his movements and slipped the package into his jacket, before locking the box.

He turned and caught one of the post office employees watching him from a doorway farther along the alleyway, her face quizzical. He forced a smile, erasing the hunted expression he knew must be etched across his face, and raised his hand in greeting, and then strode towards the street.

He hurried along the road before entering a café he and Amy frequented and sat at a table towards the back, facing the door.

Once the waitress had taken his coffee order, he reached inside his pocket and pulled out Amy's letter.

He ran his fingers over her neat handwriting, his name written in her looping script, and then ripped open the envelope and extracted a single page of notepaper.

He blinked back tears at the sight of Amy's handwriting, her message brief but to the point.

Will, they'll be after the information on one of these drives. Keep the larger one for yourself – give them the smaller one. Your copy has all my notes on it. I was so close to finding the one piece of evidence that would end Rossiter's political career and probably put him in prison for a very long time. You need to find that now. Hopefully by the time they work out it's not on the hard drive you give them, you'll have a good head start. Love you, Amy x.

Will jumped as the waitress placed his coffee in front of him and held his hand up in apology.

She smiled, shrugged, and walked away to tend to another customer.

Will read the note once more, his fingers tracing Amy's words, before he folded it and tucked it into his backpack. He pushed the larger of the two square-shaped hard drives to the bottom of the bag, then pulled out the smaller and turned it in his hands.

He was still lost in thought when his phone vibrated in his pocket, and he answered it, his heart thumping, blood rushing in his ears before he realised the caller's number had been withheld.

I'm out of time.

'H-hello?'

'You saw what we did to your friend, Will. Now – where the fuck are the files?'

Chapter 8

Immediate thoughts of denial were swept aside as Will ran his hand through his hair. His insides threatened to turn to liquid. Somehow, the caller had anticipated he'd visit Simon. Then, when the computer expert had failed to be any use, he'd been killed.

'Are you listening to me, Will?'

Will mumbled incoherently into the phone, trying to buy some time to think.

It didn't work.

'What's that? I can't hear you, Will. Don't fuck about with me. Speak up.'

'Yes. I'm listening.' He held his head in his hand, the phone pressed tightly to his ear.

'Her laptop's been wiped clean. Remember, Will. I can kill her. Just because she's in a hospital doesn't mean she's safe from me. So where the hell are the files?'

'Th-there's a hard drive.'

'Where? Do you have it?'

'Yes – but I only found out about it a minute ago.'

'You're going to bring the hard drive to me.' A pause, another cigarette inhaled.

Will waited, blood rushing in his ears. He strained to hear the caller's voice over the noise in the café and pulled the phone away from his ear to turn the volume up. The caller was talking again by the time he put the phone back.

'What? Sorry – it's busy here. I didn't get that,' Will stumbled.

'Christ.' Another drag on the cigarette. 'Stick to the plan, Will.'

'What do you mean?'

'Nothing changes. Put the hard drive in a shopping bag and leave it on the bench seat at the bus stop opposite the shopping centre. Get moving. You've got thirty minutes.'

The phone went dead. Will pulled it away from his ear and stared at it, then looked at his watch.

Thirty minutes.

Will stood, pocketed his phone, threw some change onto the table, and then raced from the café.

At a bus stop, he hailed the first double-decked vehicle that pulled up to the kerb, threw himself into a seat, and mentally worked through a route which would get him to the drop-off area in plenty of time.

As the bus pushed through traffic along the street, it drew up to another stop. Will glanced up as it slowed, then his heart lurched, and he stood, hurrying through the doors and onto the pavement.

Ten minutes later, he hailed a different bus.

As the vehicle swayed, he reached into his pocket, pulled out his mobile phone, and frowned. He'd seen it on television, but would it work? He shrugged, turned the phone over and prised open the back, then removed the battery. He put the phone back together, put the battery in the front pocket of the backpack and the phone into his pocket, then leaned back in his seat.

A quarter of a mile before the drop-off point, Will climbed from the bus, stuffed his hands in his pockets, and stalked through the entrance to a park as the vehicle pulled away from the kerb.

He followed a path into the centre of the green space, desperate for a few moments of solitude while he tried to gather his thoughts.

Before he'd pulled the battery from his phone, he'd noted the icon flashing which signified a missed call. He pulled the DCI's business card from his pocket and checked the number.

It confirmed his suspicions.

The police were trying to contact him, which meant that they'd probably found out about the break-in at the apartment, probably from an astute neighbour.

Or a tip-off.

He sank onto a bench next to the path and held his head in his hands.

What if the caller had told the police about the break-in to stop Will from returning home?

By now, he reasoned, the whole apartment would've been turned into a crime scene. And he had nowhere else to go.

He leaned back, the two hard drives in his pack sticking into his spine, and wondered what Amy had got caught up in.

Somehow, she'd uncovered a story that had some very powerful people scared. Certainly, they were scared enough that they had no qualms in attacking the favourite candidate to win the General Election and killing two men, injuring her in the process.

And then ransack his home and stalk him until he handed over some information they would most certainly kill again for if they didn't get it.

He pinched the bridge of his nose and gazed over the treeline of the park to the cityscape beyond.

Grey clouds had begun to form, another rain storm gathering strength to the south of the capital.

The wind had picked up, ruffling his hair, and he brushed it out of his eyes, noticing that the group of students who had been kicking a ball about on the grass were also packing up, pointing at the changing weather as they sauntered out of the park.

Part of him wanted to put the battery back into his phone, call the hospital, and find out how the surgery was progressing. He blinked, left the mobile phone where it was, and pulled out the smaller of the two hard drives from his backpack, turning it in his hands.

The simplest option – the best option – would be to hand over the hard drive and walk away in the hope he and Amy would be left alone, but even as the thought entered his mind, he realised that Amy's life would remain in danger.

Whatever Amy had been investigating in relation to Ian Rossiter wouldn't just disappear with the hard drive – Amy herself knew the details.

He'd have to do what Amy's note said – access the second drive and go through her notes to find something, anything, which would explain the morning's events. Something he could use once he'd handed the hard drive over to the mysterious caller. Something that person had killed Simon for, and probably the politician's driver and bodyguard, too.

He squared his shoulders with renewed determination, and fought down the panic that crawled in his gut. She knew he hated mysteries, but this time, he didn't have a choice.

Her life depended on him.

Will stood, slipped the hard drive back into his backpack, and moved away from the bench, walking out of the park and towards the drop-off point. He pulled the phone from his pocket, inserted the battery, and waited until three bars of signal appeared, closely followed by a message that he'd missed a call from a blocked number.

His heart began to beat rapidly. Maybe it had worked – maybe he really had disappeared off the grid for a while. Maybe the mystery caller was panicking. Maybe...

Will nearly dropped the phone as it began to ring.

'Hello?'

'Don't 'hello' me. Where the fuck have you been?'

Will swallowed. 'What do you mean? I'm on my way to the drop-off point.'

'Don't fuck with me, Will. She's not out of danger until I get the hard drive.'

The caller hung up.

Will put the phone back into his pocket, his hand shaking. His gaze swept the street as he began to hurry along the pavement.

He spotted the drop-off point a hundred or so paces away.

It was one of the new benches the local borough council had installed recently, a concrete base with the seat and back support comprised of black metal slats. Graffiti already covered the surface in places.

A bus shelter cocooned it from the worst of the elements, its sides plastered with posters advertising more mobile phone deals on one side and a familiar brand of dog food on the other. Evidently the sales agency knew its local demographics well.

Will checked his watch.

Two minutes.

He drew level with the bench and pretended to be interested in the photographic display in the estate agent's shop next to it.

As he looked at the adverts for houses he could never afford, he shrugged his backpack off his shoulder, shoved his hand inside, and wrapped his fingers around the smaller of the two hard drives.

'I hope you're right about this Amy,' he murmured, and then turned.

There were no passengers waiting on the bench, the seat facing the road, and when Will approached, he saw why.

A temporary sign had been placed across the timetable stating that buses wouldn't be picking up passengers from the stop until further notice.

He placed the hard drive on the seat and hurried away, re-zipping the backpack.

He took another look at his watch.

He was on time.

Will spun on his heel and desperately searched for somewhere he could hide and observe the bus stop without being seen.

His phone rang once more.

'Hello?'

'Stop hanging about, Will. Fuck off.'

The line went dead.

'Shit.'

The road began to curve as he hurried past the shopping centre on the opposite side of the road, trying to put as much distance as he could between him and the drop-off point.

A car honked its horn behind him, cutting through the noise of the traffic and sending his heartbeat racing.

When he turned, a bus had drawn to a halt at the bus stop, its engine idling, blocking his view of the bench seat.

His mind raced. He spun round, peering up at the buildings that towered over the street. The caller was evidently watching him – or had people in position to keep an eye on his every movement. What if something went wrong? Should he check the hard drive was still there? What if a passenger picked it up by mistake, and handed it in to the police?

Will cursed, walked a few paces, reached a pedestrian crossing, and hit the button.

'Come on!' he hissed under his breath. He punched the button again, his mouth dry. Every instinct told him to run, to get away from the caller and his people, but he had to know. He had to find out if the hard drive was in the right hands and that Amy would be safe, for now.

A taxi streaked over the pedestrian crossing moments before the zap of the timer kicked in and the little green man icon on the opposite side of the road lit up.

Will was elbowed to one side, and a man hurried past him.

'Out of the way,' he growled, a phone to his ear as he stalked across the road.

'Sorry,' said Will, and then heard a hiss from the bus.

His head jerked right, just in time to see the doors shut.

The vehicle's engine rumbled up a notch, and then the bus pulled away from the kerb.

Will craned his neck.

There was no one walking away from or towards him.

He spun round to see where the man with the mobile phone had gone, his thoughts racing, before he saw him farther along the pavement, next to a woman with a push-chair, grinning as he hoisted a toddler into the air and hugged him.

His heart pounding, he ran back across the road, dodging a car, and hurried back to the bench as the red double-decker passed him, walking in the opposite direction.

He already knew what he'd find when he reached the bench.

Nothing.

He glanced over his shoulder to see the bus slowly disappearing along the busy street, black smoke spewing from its exhaust.

His gaze fell to the timetable.

The temporary notice had gone.

'Shit.'

The collector had been on the bus, and he'd missed his only chance to try to see who he was dealing with.

He kicked the side of the bus shelter, disgusted with himself, then retraced his steps along the pavement, intent on finding the nearest underground station.

Now he had no choice. He had to find out what was on the second hard drive.

Before the caller discovered that his copy was incomplete.

Chapter 9

Malcolm Gregory drummed his fingers on the desk, then reached to his lips, extracted the dying cigarette, and stubbed it out in the ashtray in front of him.

The day's events had been troubling.

They had been caught out when the reporter had first called last week and insisted on a meeting at short notice. The office had descended into a frenzy, trying to fathom what she might have uncovered, wrongly assuming it was the usual tabloid dirt that circled Westminster in the weeks leading up to an election.

Despite advertising a partisan outlook to their readers, the lower market newspapers could always be relied upon to assist where necessary, and it was with this in mind that Gregory had agreed to the meeting, although he'd pulled rank and insisted it take place on neutral territory.

The reporter had agreed, a little too eagerly, and the appropriate arrangements had been made.

He tapped the delicately embossed cigarette lighter on the mahogany surface.

In hindsight, his insistence that the meeting not take place immediately had been prescient. With less than a week to prepare, he'd used his most trusted people to follow the woman, track her movements, and attempt to pre-empt the contents of her investigation.

She'd been clever, though, hiding information, avoiding emailing anything to her editor. For all Gregory and his team could find, she'd been working alone on her story.

What his team did uncover at the last minute, only a day away from the scheduled interview, led to one of the most gruelling twenty-four hours he'd ever known.

He'd instructed Rossiter to send all but the most trusted staff home, then sealed off his room and explained to the man what was going to happen if they didn't control the situation immediately.

Rossiter had reacted exactly as he'd anticipated.

He raised his eyes to the stain on the wall, a chunk of plaster missing where the man had thrown his brandy glass at the surface, shards of glass exploding across the leather sofa underneath.

Gregory had stood sentinel in the middle of the room, unmoving, his hands clasped behind his back as Rossiter had shouted, cursed, and paced, until eventually he had calmed down, sunk into one of the chairs beside the desk, and held his head in his hands, asking Gregory for his advice.

As he always had.

His eyes moved to the chess board on the small table in front of the sofa. Of course, he'd been planning. Had been since the reporter's initial request. Contingencies, strategies, counter-strategies. It was a skill he'd honed over the years, plotting and coercing people like the pieces on the board.

Rossiter had listened to his plan as he'd calmly described it and remained silent while his colleague had talked.

Gregory had paused halfway through his narrative to take a delicate sip from his own brandy and ignored the man in front of him who had obviously wished he hadn't thrown his own against the wall by the way he licked his lips then looked away. Gregory had managed to contain the shudder of pleasure that worked its way through him at the man's discomfort, before continuing to set out what would need to take place the next day.

A silence had fallen over the room when he'd finished, and he'd wondered for a moment whether he'd gone too far, tested the party leader's resolve too much.

He needn't have worried.

Rossiter had rubbed his hand over his face, and then stalked across the room to the decanter and poured himself a large measure into a fresh glass. He'd thrown half of it down his throat before making his decision.

Gregory exhaled and ran his hand over his head.

It was his job to protect Rossiter, to make sure the man's ambitions were realised. The reporter's investigation had warranted extreme measures; he had to believe that. He *did* believe it.

His hand hovered above the mobile phone, before he snatched it back and took a deep breath, chastising himself. More than one phone call a day to the hospital to discuss her condition would seem strange.

He had to remain calm, at least until his security team returned with the computer hard drive and its contents assessed.

He shook his head and cursed their incompetence. The man was an archivist, for goodness' sake, not a spy. Yet, somehow, he'd managed to evade them since dropping off the hard drive as instructed.

He rubbed his chin, then lifted the receiver for the internal phone and dialled a number. The recipient answered within two rings. Gregory didn't wait for a greeting.

'Have you got it yet?'

'Yes. There's a lot of data here to go through.'

'I don't need excuses. I need results. Today.'

'It'll be much later than that. There's no logical order to how the files have been saved. It'll be tomorrow at the earliest. We should have an idea what we've got here by then.'

'Make sure you do.'

Gregory slammed the phone down and slumped in his chair, then pulled a piece of paper across the desk towards him and unfolded it. The name and address of a nursing home had been scrawled across the page.

At the moment, Rossiter wasn't aware of the details, but Gregory felt that a contingency plan should be in place, just in case.

He glanced up at a knock at his door, folded the page, and tucked it into the inside pocket of his jacket as a woman entered.

'Excuse me, sir? Mr Rossiter would like to speak with you now. The secure line in the private meeting room.' She grasped the leather-bound briefing folder in one hand and used an expensive-looking pen to scribble notes as she spoke.

'Can't it wait?'

The woman stared at him incredulously, as if he'd suggested sleeping with her. Rossiter didn't wait for anyone and was well known for his short temper amongst the staff.

'He said it was urgent.'

Gregory sighed. 'Very well. Lead the way, Alison.'

Chapter 10

‘Will? What are you doing here?’ Russell jumped up from his chair and strode across the room. ‘Shouldn’t you be home, or at the hospital, or…’

‘Probably. I need your help, though.’ Will glanced around the room, the IT department’s floor covered with spare computer monitors and hard drives. Two graduate IT specialists sat at their desks, their faces turned towards him. ‘Is there somewhere more private where we can talk?’

‘Sure.’

Will followed Russell across the open-plan office until they reached a small room set off to one side.

‘My manager’s on annual leave, so we can use his office.’ Russell flicked a light switch and pulled out two chairs from under a glass-topped desk. 'Here – sit down.'

Will dropped into the chair and put the backpack between his feet.

'How is she?'

Will shrugged and checked his phone. 'Still in surgery. They're going to phone me when they know something more.'

Russell nodded, and Will realised no one knew what to say to him about Amy. They were all lost for words.

He decided to launch straight into his idea. 'Russ, can I use your computer?'

The other man shrugged. 'I suppose. Where's yours?'

Will leaned down and pulled the second hard drive from his bag. 'I can't go back to the apartment at the moment.'

'Why not?'

Will ran his hand through his hair, and then exhaled. He had nothing to hide from Russell, but he needed to be careful. 'While I was at the hospital, the apartment was broken into.'

'What? Have you told the police?'

Will ignored the question and instead held up the hard drive and turned it to face his friend. 'I think Amy has some files on here, and I'd like to see what's on them.'

'What sort of files?'

Will glanced over his shoulder, then stood and closed the office door. He returned to his chair and hugged the hard drive against his chest. 'Some very important files.' He raised his gaze to Russell, who was staring at him, worry creasing his brow. 'Files that someone might harm people to get.'

Silence filled the room, the sound of the wall clock filling the air. Eventually, Russell leaned forward in his chair, rested his elbows on his knees, and exhaled.

'Do you think this is why Amy was shot?'

Will nodded.

'And you think someone ransacked your apartment trying to find it?

'Yes.'

'And this is why you can't go back home?'

'Exactly.'

Russell eased back, held his hands to his lips as if in silent prayer, and then held out his hand. 'Give me the hard drive. Let's see what we can find.'

While his colleague connected the hard drive to his computer, Will stepped away and moved over to the window. Resting his forehead against the glass, he peered down at the gridlocked traffic moving along Montague Place.

'There's something else you need to know, Russ.'

'What?'

'I've got to work through whatever's on that hard drive to stop what's happening. If I don't, they're going to kill Amy. Even if she survives surgery, they'll get to her.'

He closed his eyes as Russell cursed.

'Have you told the police?'

'No. Not yet.' He turned to face his friend.

'What are you going to do?'

Will pointed at the hard drive. 'Whoever did it was after that. Or what's on it, at least.' He leaned against the window sill, before folding his arms across his chest. 'A man phoned me on our landline while I was at the apartment. He said I had to bring

Amy's laptop to him.' He held out the notepaper with the scrawled instructions on it, his hand shaking.

Russell snatched it from him. 'What did you do?'

'I – I told him I had to go and get it. I had to collect the laptop from our computer expert, because Amy was having an upgrade done to it.' Will turned away and wiped his eyes. 'I phoned ahead to our computer guy and told him I needed to take a look for the files.' He sniffled. 'When I got there, he was dead. The police were crawling all over the place. One of the neighbours told me it sounded like a robbery gone wrong.'

'Jesus, Will.' Russell's eyes opened wide, his jaw slack. 'What the bloody hell is going on?'

'I don't know,' said Will. 'But whatever it is, Amy's life depends on it. The police interviewed me at the hospital. They haven't got a clue who attacked Amy, so they can't guarantee her safety, can they?' He pointed at the hard drive. 'But, maybe – if I can access the files she's got on there – I can find out who they are and stop them.'

'Will, if you find out who's doing this, go to the police with that information,' said Russell. 'No fucking about either, got that?'

'Okay.'

'Did anyone follow you here?'

'I don't know – but even if they did, they're probably thinking I have to clear the time off with Jack to look after Amy and sort this mess out, right? I mean, I don't think you're in danger, okay?'

'You don't *think*?' Russell raised his gaze to the ceiling. 'Bloody hell, Will.'

'Can you open the files for me?' said Will. 'I need to know what I'm dealing with. Amy's messages didn't tell me. I think she ran out of time.'

The computer engineer leaned forward, his fingers jabbing at the keyboard in front of him. 'I can try. We sometimes have to access people's computers here if they're off sick or go on holiday and forget to put their files on the shared server, so I'd imagine it'll be a similar process. Give me a minute or two.'

Will glanced down after his mobile phone began to ring and recognised the number as that of the hospital switchboard.

'I need to take this,' he said.

‘Sure – use the office next door. It’s empty.’

‘Thanks.’

He left Russell scrolling through the files, opening an occasional one to gauge its content, and closed the door before answering the phone.

‘Will Fletcher.’

‘Mr Fletcher, this is the Prince George Hospital. Please hold the line. I’ll connect you to Mr Hathaway,’ said the receptionist.

Will pushed open the door to the abandoned office, switched on the lights, and sank into a worn swivel chair while the dulcet tones of Faure’s *Berceuse* filtered down the line.

He swung round on the chair as he waited, the bare walls offering no clue as to the role of its previous occupant, save for a calendar depicting an autumn scene, the page turned to a date six months earlier.

There was no window in the room, and Will had begun to loosen his collar to counteract the stuffiness, when the surgeon’s voice cut into the music.

‘Hello, Will.’

'Hi.' Will tried to detect from the tone of the man's voice how Amy's operation had gone and quickly gave up. 'How is she?'

The surgeon sighed, and Will heard the squeak of the man's chair as he moved.

'The procedure went well,' he said. 'I'm satisfied we've done all we can at this stage.'

'But?'

'It's very early to be speculating, Will. There's an incredible amount of trauma and bruising to her skull, as you can imagine.' He cleared his throat. 'I noticed during the surgery that she has a scar above her eyebrow – an old injury,' he said. 'Do you know anything about that?'

'Not really – I think she hit her head as a kid and needed stitches.'

'Okay, good to know,' said the surgeon. 'I don't think it's going to cause us any additional problems with her recovery.'

'So, what happens now?' Will leaned back in his chair and stared at the ceiling. A cobweb floated in the breeze from the air conditioning vent, and he hugged his arm across his chest, stuffing his hand under his arm to try and stop the shaking in his limbs.

'We simply have to wait,' said Hathaway. 'We'll be monitoring her constantly, but you need to understand, it could be days, rather than hours, before I can give you an indication of her prognosis.'

'What do I do now?'

'Stay by the phone, and keep in touch,' said the surgeon. 'If you'd like to come in and sit with her for a while, let my secretary know, and she'll make the necessary arrangements.'

Will leaned forward and pressed the phone closer to his ear. 'I'll do that,' he said. I've just got some things to sort out first.'

'I understand,' said the surgeon, and Will heard the note of disappointment in his voice.

Hathaway continued. 'I'll ensure we phone you every few hours with an update, even if it's just to say there's no change. I've also been asked to notify the police the moment Amy regains consciousness,' he said. 'But you'll be the first to hear anything. I'll make sure of that.'

'Thank you,' said Will.

He ended the call and wiped his eyes, composing himself before leaving the empty office and returning to the meeting room. He pushed open the door, closing it quietly behind him.

Russell stood by the window, hands in his pockets, his spine stiff. He turned as Will entered the room, his face pale.

'What is it?' asked Will. 'Are you okay?'

'Not really. No,' said Russell. 'This doesn't look like a newspaper story, Will. This is obsessive. It's like she's got a personal vendetta or something.' He pointed at his laptop. 'What do you make of that?'

Will strode over to the desk and spun the computer round. On it, an enlarged black and white photograph filled the screen.

A group of four men stood in a row, their hairstyles short, clipped close to their skulls. Two wore camouflage-printed clothes and lace-up ankle height boots in a dark colour. The others appeared to be wearing jeans and long-sleeved dark sweatshirts, with no logos.

Will frowned. 'Not much. Four blokes. Two in army fatigues. All looking a bit smug.'

Russell's fingers swept across the keyboard, until the top right hand corner of the picture was enlarged. He spun the screen round to face Will.

'Now tell me what you see,' he whispered. 'Look closer.'

Will's hands trembled as he pulled the laptop nearer. He peered at the photograph, and then pulled out one of the chairs, sitting down heavily. He rubbed his hands over his knees in an attempt to stop his legs from shaking.

'How is that even possible?' he said. 'Can you get this photo cleaned up? I mean, I know what I *think* I'm seeing, but it's not exactly conclusive evidence, is it? It's too blurred.'

'I could take a copy of this file. See if one of the IT guys can do something with it, if you like?'

Will thought for a second, the image of Simon's body being carried away on a stretcher fresh in his mind. *But if they were right…*

'Can he be trusted not to tell anyone else?'

'Yeah – he's good.'

'Okay. Do it,' said Will. He rubbed his hand over his eyes. 'What's going on, Russ? What do you think this all means?'

'I think it means you're in a lot more trouble than you realise.'

Chapter 11

Will replaced the petrol cap on the old four-door sedan and walked across the garage forecourt to the pay point.

An hour earlier, he'd managed to persuade Russell to loan him his car. His friend had handed over the keys reluctantly.

Russell's eyes had narrowed. 'How long?'

'Just for a couple of days.'

'Are you sure?' asked Russell. 'I mean, don't take this the wrong way, but your girlfriend's in an induced coma – and you're planning to leave town?'

'I've got nowhere else to go,' said Will. He held up his hand. 'I'm not staying with you or any other friends. It's too dangerous.' He held up the hard drive before slipping it into his backpack. 'I need to hide, keep my head down for a day or two – give me time to work out what all this means.'

'Take it to the police.'

'I can't. Don't you see? It could take weeks for them to work this out. I don't have weeks, Russ. I need to do this now – before these people find out Amy left behind *two* hard drives.' He held out his hand. 'Give me your car keys. Please.'

'You hate driving.'

'I can't rely on public transport at the moment.'

'You're a crap driver.'

'I'll be okay.'

'You hate motorways.'

'Russ – please! I don't have time for this!'

Will had held his breath as his friend glared at him, eventually pulling his keys from his pocket and tossing them to him.

'It's parked at Lewisham station. Watch the gearbox – it's a bit sticky in third.'

'Thanks.'

'Be careful,' said Russell. 'I've got no idea what you're getting yourself into, but I know it's not good.'

Will had pulled the door open, and then turned back to the room. 'I'll see you in a couple of days, okay?'

He'd reached Lewisham, collected the car, and on the way out of town, pulled up outside an office supplies store belonging to a large retail chain that sold computers as well as the more mundane stationery.

He'd purchased a cheap laptop and a small desk printer, before hurrying back to the borrowed vehicle.

Now, the futility of what he was hoping to achieve clouded his thoughts.

At Russell's suggestion, they'd gone into a branch of a bank near to the museum and had withdrawn a large sum of cash from Russell's account.

'If they were watching your apartment, they might be monitoring your bank and credit cards too,' his friend had pointed out.

Will had to admit he had a fair point. The irony of the fact that he was spending his and Amy's hard-earned house deposit wasn't lost on him, either.

In the space of mere hours, their lives had been turned upside down.

He frowned. The more he thought about it, the more it appeared that Amy had been preparing for something to happen.

A polite cough jolted him back to the present, and he mumbled an apology to the person standing behind him and shuffled up to the cashier's window.

'Pump number four, please.'

He handed over some notes, waited for his change, and then hurried from the service station and across the forecourt to the café.

As soon as he walked through the door, he made his way over to the coffee vending machine. While he waited for the thick viscous liquid to pour, he pulled out his phone, replaced the battery, and noticed two new voicemail messages waiting for him.

He reached over the counter for a napkin and a pen and hastily scribbled down the messages – one from the hospital and the other from DCI Lake.

As soon as he had finished, his paranoia still piqued by the events of the day, he ripped the battery from the phone once more, and then glanced around the café until he saw a sign for a payphone.

The coffee machine whirred, and the last of the brown liquid spluttered into the cardboard cup. Will grabbed a takeaway lid and hurried across to the telephone.

The policeman's gruff tones answered within seconds.

'Lake.'

'It's Will Fletcher.'

'We've been trying to reach you, Will.'

'Yeah, sorry – I had to leave town. My mother is ill. Have you found out who shot Amy?'

He heard the policeman cover the phone and talk to someone before he returned to the call.

'Sorry about that, Will. I just had someone with me,' he said. 'We're still pursuing enquiries at the moment, but I wanted to talk to you about something else. Have you been back to the apartment since we spoke?'

Will crossed his fingers. 'No – I went back into work to sort some stuff out, then had to leave town.'

'Ah, I see. Will, there's no easy way to tell you this, but your apartment was broken into.'

Will remained quiet, letting the silence stretch a while before speaking. 'What do you mean 'broken into'? Has anything been taken?'

'It doesn't look like it at first glance,' said the detective. 'Any valuable goods that might have been seized, such as your television, are still there. Unfortunately, though, the place has been torn apart – as if someone was looking for something.'

'Wow. When did that happen?'

'We've narrowed down the time between eleven and one o'clock.'

Twelve forty-five actually, thought Will. *I nearly walked in on the intruder.*

He recalled the out-of-service elevator and the whirring of the machinery as it began its downward descent while he'd climbed the stairs.

'What happens now?'

'Well, forensics have finished – I tried to phone you as soon as we found out about it. Took uniform a while to get word to us, and then we put two and two together and realised it was yours and Amy's apartment. Our team arrived at four o'clock.'

'Sorry – my phone's been switched off. Forgot my battery charger.'

Will bit his lip. He couldn't think of anything to say to the detective that wouldn't cause him problems.

Such as why he was standing next to a motorway in the middle of Surrey, trying to fathom why his girlfriend had been shot. Or why he was scared of a mystery man who phoned him on a regular basis demanding that he hand over Amy's investigative notes.

He waited another heartbeat and then spoke. 'What's happening now? Is the apartment secure?'

The policeman sighed. 'Yes, we got a locksmith in while forensics were there. Your neighbour, a Mrs Hegarty, has the keys. She was the one that dialled 999 when she discovered the break-in.'

Before Will wondered whether he should offer any more information, the detective spoke again.

'Look, Will – the apartment's secure now. If you've got things to sort out with family, I understand – but I do need you to check your messages more often. Where are you, anyway?'

Will swallowed. 'I'm, um, I'm staying with a distant relative in Surrey at the moment, so I'm only a few hours' away if you need me. My mother's ill.' He coughed. 'How's Mr Rossiter getting on?'

The detective lowered his voice. 'He was discharged an hour ago, Will. At his own request.'

'Lucky bastard.' Will ran his hand over his eyes, then pinched the bridge of his nose. 'Was he able to tell you anything about the attack?'

'I'm sorry. I'm not at liberty to discuss that with you, Will. You know that.' The detective sighed. 'I'll keep you up to date on progress as much as I can, but there's a lot of information we're working through at the moment, as you can understand.'

Will cleared his throat. 'I understand. Sorry, but I have to go.'

'Right, well, let me know as soon as you're back in town. I'd prefer it if you came to the station first before going to the apartment, just so I can go through some paperwork with you, all right?'

'Okay.'

Will disconnected the call, his heart thumping. He chewed his thumbnail and wondered what his next steps were.

First of all, he had to find somewhere to stay. He plucked a booklet from a display next to the payphone, its cover advertising a motel chain prevalent in the area, and hurried back out to the car clutching his coffee.

As he pulled away into the traffic driving north, he looked at the shopping bag on the passenger seat. His next task would be to read through the rest of Amy's notes on the hard drive.

Some twenty miles farther down the road, he pulled into the car park of one of the motel chain's premises, switched off the engine, and stared across at the reception area.

The sky was beginning to darken and an earlier weather report had suggested rain.

As he looked towards the reception area, he saw a sign next to the front door.

No cash accepted.

He realised he wouldn't be able to use his credit card here, either.

'Shit.'

He rummaged in his backpack, until he found Amy's phone and switched it on, typing in the familiar phone number.

'Russ? It's me. Can you do me a favour?'

Five minutes later, Will climbed out the vehicle, pulled the laptop and his backpack from the seat next to him, and locked the car.

He hurried across the car park as the first drops of rain began to splash on the asphalt at his feet and reached the portico of the motel's entrance. He took a deep breath and pushed against the glass front door.

A female receptionist looked up from her computer screen as he entered.

'Good afternoon, sir.'

'Hi,' said Will and approached the desk. He lowered his backpack to his feet. 'I believe my research assistant just phoned through with a reservation for me? My name's Will Fletcher.'

A smile crossed the woman's face. 'He certainly did. Some sort of mix-up with your other hotel, is that right?'

'Yes. Last time we use them.' He grinned. 'I guess we should've thought of coming here in the first place.'

The receptionist smiled politely as she typed at her keyboard. 'You'll just have to bear us in mind in future,' she said. 'Now, your assistant's paid for the room and has left credit card details as a guarantee for any purchases while you're here, so all I need from you today is your driver's licence.'

Will extracted his wallet and handed over his licence. After discussing it with Russell, they'd agreed that it was probably safe to do so, given that Russell's credit card was being used for the actual room purchase.

He waited while the receptionist disappeared into a back office to photocopy his licence and tried not to let his impatience show before she returned and gave him instructions on where to park his car while he was staying at the motel.

After moving the car to the back of the complex, he hurried across the car park to the smaller guest entrance and followed the signs on the walls to his room.

The passageway meandered through twists and turns, and he had almost convinced himself he was walking in the wrong direction when he spotted the door to his allocated room.

Swiping his card, he entered the room, locked the door behind him, and dumped his backpack on the double bed.

The window faced out onto the front entrance and the main road, a net curtain providing privacy from the gloomy afternoon outside.

He switched on the small plastic kettle, then pulled out the hard drive and new laptop and began to set everything up on the small desk.

Once he could delay no longer, he took some calming breaths before picking up the room phone and dialling the number for the hospital.

'Hi – it's Will Fletcher here. I was wondering if I could speak to Mr Hathaway please. I'm returning his call.'

He drummed his fingers on the desk while he waited for the surgeon to come to the phone and was surprised when a female voice carried down the line.

'Hello, Will. This is Susan Phillips – I'm the charge nurse on the ward tonight. Thanks for calling back.'

'How is she?'

'No change at the moment – we just wanted to give you an update and let you know that Mr Hathaway has reviewed the CT scans we ran after the surgery,' the nurse continued. 'He's pleased with how the operation went, but wanted me to impress upon you that it's still early days.'

Will heard another voice in the background and changed tack. 'Okay, well, I'll be checking my messages regularly, so please, as soon as you can tell me anything, let me know.'

'Of course, Will,' the nurse said. 'Just remember that the next forty-eight hours are going to be critical.'

'They sure are,' said Will and replaced the phone in its cradle.

Chapter 12

Will sat up in bed, flicked absently through the television channels with the remote control, and watched the dawn light begin to prise its fingers through the faded material of the closed curtains at the window.

He'd fallen into an exhausted sleep within moments of ending the call to the hospital, drained emotionally from the events of the past day.

At two o'clock in the morning, he'd awoken suddenly, jolted out of a nightmare in which he'd been running towards a black sedan parked skewed in the middle of a busy street. As people had walked past its opened doors, he'd run to the car and bent down to the back seat to see Amy staring at him, the small scar on her forehead now bloody and raw.

She'd been holding the hard drive out to him, her eyes desperate, her mouth working soundlessly.

He'd rolled over, wiped the sweat from his forehead, and pushed back the blankets, before switching on the television and muting the sound. Sleep would not return that night.

Rolling reports on the twenty-four hour television news channel repeated every half hour, and Will lost count how many times he'd seen the footage of Rossiter's car. He'd turned the volume up half an hour ago when he'd heard the person in the neighbouring room get into the shower.

He pulled the blankets up closer round his shoulders and swapped the remote control to his left hand so he could warm up the fingers of his right.

His gaze flickered back to the screen as the newsreader perked up and stated that an immediate announcement would be made by Ian Rossiter's office.

The picture on the television changed to show a woman standing outside the House of Commons. Despite the hour, the reporter's shoulder-length brown hair was perfectly styled, her make-up precise, and her business suit expensive.

The in-studio newsreader spoke first. 'So, Stacey, Mr Rossiter's office has just released a statement, is that correct?'

Stacey squinted slightly in the bright lights of the television cameras before speaking.

'That's right, Hannah,' she said. 'Mr Rossiter's press secretary has issued a brief press release stating that the political candidate will be holding a press conference at his home later today, where he is currently recovering from his wounds.'

Will snorted.

'Do you think Mr Rossiter will use the press conference to give us some idea as to why he was attacked?'

Will frowned as the newsreader tried, and failed, to hide her glee at the prospect, before the reporter spoke once more.

'At this time, it's unknown what the exact content of his press conference will be,' she said, 'However, there is a lot of speculation here at his candidacy office that he will tell us some more about what happened yesterday morning and what the police are doing to trace the perpetrators of this vicious crime.'

'Indeed, thank you,' said the newsreader, before the outside broadcast feed disappeared. 'Stacey Greaves there with that report,' she continued. 'Of course, as soon as we have more details about that press conference, we'll let you know. Now, onto other news…'

Will turned the volume off and rubbed his hands over his eyes, before kicking back the blankets.

He switched on the air-conditioning and adjusted the temperature controls, then hurried to the shower to stand under the warm water.

When he returned to the bedroom rubbing a towel over his damp hair, the room was warmer and he dressed in the jeans and sweatshirt he'd purchased the previous afternoon, along with the toiletries that now lay strewn around the small bathroom.

He switched on the new laptop and made a mug of tea while he waited for it to complete its start-up activities.

He raised the mug to his lips and paused.

'Genius,' he murmured.

He switched on Amy's mobile phone and scrolled through her contacts list until he found the number he sought. He switched the mobile back off, and then using the motel's landline, he dialled the number and waited, the ring tone beating a rhythm to the idea going round in his mind.

When the call was answered, he took a deep breath before speaking. 'Kirby? It's Will Fletcher. Hi. No – no news yet. She's out of surgery and in intensive care. I'm waiting for them to phone with an update.'

He paused while Amy's editor made small talk about his protégé's condition, before pushing ahead with his idea. 'Kirby? Ian Rossiter's having a press conference this afternoon. Yes – at his house. I was wondering, hope you don't mind my asking, would you be able to get me on the press list for it?'

Will held his breath as the silence at the other end of the line drew out a little longer than he would have liked, before Amy's boss responded.

'No – I won't be asking any questions or making a nuisance of myself. I'd just like to hear first-hand what happened.' He sniffled and wiped his eyes. 'I'm having trouble making sense of it all, to be honest.'

He waited, his heart hammering against his ribs.

'Really? That's great – thanks very much. Yes, I'll stay out of the way of your reporter. Of course –

if I hear anything, I'll be sure to give you a call. Thanks again. Bye.'

He ended the call and punched the air.

He hadn't lied about his reasons for wanting to attend the press conference, but there was a niggling thought he couldn't shake. Something to do with Amy's research and the timing of the attack.

He exhaled, tipped the rest of the tea down his throat, and pulled out a chair to begin going through the files on the external hard drive once more.

Will opened the first of the folders saved to the hard drive. Each had been saved with a date as the file name, making it easy to read through the documents in chronological order.

Next, Will opened up a second folder of documents. This time, three video clips were saved, again by date in chronological order. He pulled out a set of headphones from his backpack, cursed as he tried to untangle the coiled lead, then put them in his ears and hit 'play' on the first file.

A new report from a few months ago started. Will sat up straight. He remembered this – he and Amy had seen it at the apartment. Ian Rossiter had announced his intention to run for the leadership of his political party after the previous incumbent had died suddenly of a heart attack, and the media had gone wild. Amy had scooted her butt across the sofa, snatched the television remote out of Will's hand, turned up the volume and had sat, transfixed at the screen while the report played out.

So why was she so interested? And why was there a copy of the report here?

Will rubbed his chin, ignoring the stubble that scratched his fingers. After the news report ended, he stared at the blank screen, trying to remember. Did Amy begin her investigation into Ian Rossiter before his announcement, or did his announcement trigger her interest?

Prior to the announcement, the majority of the general public had never heard of Ian Rossiter – he'd been a minor player in a majority party, hidden somewhere on the back-bench of the government and tucked away at weekends in his small Surrey constituency.

With the death of a fellow party member who had been tipped to win at the next General Election only months away, Rossiter was seemingly plucked from obscurity to lead the party to victory.

His peers had made no secret of the fact that Rossiter's background as an accomplished businessman within the construction industry led to their choice, citing that his business success would effortlessly translate to leading a country still struggling to find its way out of a recession.

Will leaned forward, checked the date on the file, and exhaled.

Amy's interest in Ian Rossiter had been piqued right after the announcement.

He remembered now. Her excitement at going into the office the next day. Her assertion that she finally had a story that Kirby would let her run with. On her own. Except there was still a part of her which was unsure – which was why she hadn't told Will exactly what she was up to.

He hit the 'play' button on the next two video files, one after the other, but they only contained similar coverage from different television stations.

He sighed and opened up the final folder.

The last files were copies of newspaper clippings that had been scanned. One included a blurred photograph of a man bending down next to a white car, talking through the driver's window to someone unidentified, the person's features shielded by the sun's reflection on the windscreen.

Will opened up the file for the photograph he and Russell had found yesterday. Sure enough, the man in the first photograph bending down to the white car was also in the picture of the group of men in army fatigues.

He pulled back up the photo of the man standing next to the white car, and then frowned.

A shop stood behind the car, its name blurred in the background. He tried to read the name, then leaned back in his chair in surprise, realising he hadn't noticed it before.

The wording on the shop was foreign. He wracked his memory, trying to think where he'd seen writing like that on the news, and then began searching through Amy's notes for a clue. After half an hour, he found it.

Chechnya.

So the photograph had been taken sometime before the end of that particular civil war – 2003, or thereabouts.

He ran his hand over his chin, then leaned his elbow on the desk and stared at the photograph.

What the hell was going on?

He began sifting through the files in the folder with the photograph, his gaze skimming over the concise typed words Amy had entered, while his memory of her voice filled his mind.

As he scrolled through the different file types, his gaze fell on an image filename extension, and he clicked on it, his throat dry.

When it opened, it filled the entire screen, and he frowned.

The file had opened to reveal a third photograph. The image was in black and white and showed a group of men all standing facing the camera, pint jugs in hand. They were laughing and grinning at the camera, six of them in total.

Will scratched his ear lobe, and then enlarged the photograph until he could see the men's faces more clearly. His eyes moved left to right as he leaned closer, but he recognised none of them.

Frustrated, he zoomed the image back out to its original size, and then noticed a typed caption at the footer.

Annual Darts Competition Champions, Green Dragon Pub, Bracklewood.

The photograph now made some sort of sense. The men were standing in what appeared to be the pub's beer garden, celebrating their success.

'But what's the connection?'

Will exhaled and leaned back in the chair, fighting down his frustration.

He tapped his finger on the mouse button, absently moving in and out of the photograph while he went over in his mind what he'd learned.

Rossiter appeared in an old photograph with three other men, two dressed in camouflage-style clothing.

One of those men had turned up in Chechnya.

And a village darts team had won a local competition and had celebrated in the winning pub's beer garden, much to the bemused expressions of the other patrons.

The other patrons.

Will blinked and jerked forward on his chair. He scrolled the mouse until the image was enlarged once more, and then began scanning his eyes over the faces of the other people in the beer garden.

It took him another five minutes of tweaking the contrast and brightness of the picture, but eventually, he found him.

The same man from the first two photographs was sat hunched over a pint glass at one of the picnic tables in the beer garden. He was scowling, apparently displeased at being photographed. His hair was slightly longer, his fringe almost covering his eyes, but Will was certain.

Amy had found a third photograph of the mysterious man.

The name of the village in the caption sounded familiar to Will, and he opened up an internet connection on the laptop and typed in some text to find a map.

His heartbeat began to race as he skimmed through the search results, an idea forming in his mind.

Maybe the person in the newspaper clippings was still living near the pub. Maybe he'd have some ideas why Amy had been shot. Perhaps if he could get in touch with the man, he'd be able to tell Will what was really going on.

He glanced at his watch. According to the pub's website, it was only an hour's drive from Rossiter's house.

He chewed his lip and stared at the business card given to him by the DCI, debating whether to call him.

Except, if he contacted the police, the mysterious caller had threatened to kill Amy.

He picked up the card, turned it between his fingers, and then slipped it back into his pocket.

He shut down the laptop, removed the hard drive and tucked it into his backpack, then hurried from the room, hanging the 'do not disturb' sign on the outer door handle and making his way to the car.

Chapter 13

An hour and a half later, grateful for the light traffic on the road, Will turned off the engine and peered through the windscreen at the thatched roof of the pub, before climbing out and locking the vehicle.

The pub was an impressive building, set back from the road with a wide expanse of lawn leading from its front entrance down to the road, the car park off to the left, separated from the garden by a towering privet hedge.

Will pushed through a wooden gate set into the hedge and made his way along a gravel path that ran around the side of the building to the front door.

The pub appeared to be well-maintained and flourishing from its local patronage. The thatched roof was in good condition, window sills were freshly painted and baskets of early geraniums hung from steel brackets set into the whitewashed brickwork.

Across the grassed area an assortment of wooden benches and tables had been arranged and Will pulled out a copy of the photograph he'd stopped to have printed out at an office supplies store he'd spotted on his journey from the motel.

He stopped and held it up, trying to gauge where the mysterious man had sat, until he realised the idea was futile – the landlord had obviously relocated the outdoor furniture several times in the intervening years to allow the grass to grow back.

He shoved the photograph back into his pocket, checked his watch, and then trudged into the pub.

As he pushed open the door, the familiar aroma of real ale and a hint of wood smoke filled his senses. Classical music filtered through concealed speakers, and he blinked while his eyes adjusted to the subdued interior.

A man appeared at a doorway behind the bar, wiping his hands on a tea towel.

'Morning,' he said. 'What can I get for you?'

Will made his way to the polished wooden bar and glanced at the clips fastened to the four beer pumps set into the surface.

'What do the locals drink?'

'This one,' said the barman, tapping the top of a clip. 'It's our most popular beer.'

'I'll have half a pint, thanks.'

Will pulled out one of the cushioned bar stools, sat, and lowered his backpack to the floor between his feet.

Handing Will his drink and taking his money, the man turned to the till, then passed him his change.

'Just travelling through?' he asked.

Will took a gulp of his beer. 'Sort of,' he said. He put down his glass and reached into his pocket, unfolded the copy of the photograph, and pushed it across the bar. 'Were you here when this was taken?'

The landlord reached over and picked up the photo, turning it under the light from the overhang of the bar.

He smiled. 'Yes,' he said. 'I was the photographer.' He flapped the print between his fingers. 'The local newspaper bought the print off me because their photographer couldn't make it.'

Will held out his hand and introduced himself.

'Len Wilson,' said the landlord. He slid the photograph back towards Will. 'What's your interest in that? Looking up one of the darts team members, are you?'

'Actually, I was wondering if you knew who the man in the background is,' said Will. 'The one sitting on his own, there.'

He jabbed at the image.

Len reached into the top pocket of his shirt, extracted a pair of reading glasses, and slipped them on before picking up the photograph once more. He grunted, and then peered over his glasses at Will, his brow creased.

'Now,' he said. 'What could you possibly want with him?'

'Do you know him?' exclaimed Will. 'What's his name? Do you know where I can find him?'

Len handed the photograph back. 'Go and see Reverend Swift up at the church,' he said, checking his watch. 'There's a footpath from the car park you could use, but you're probably better off driving there – otherwise you'll miss him; he usually heads over to the next village for a committee meeting this time of the week.'

'Okay,' said Will, draining his glass. 'But what am I asking him?'

'Tell him I sent you, and that you're looking for Colin Avery,' said Len. 'He'll be able to point you in the right direction.'

'Great – thanks,' said Will. He grabbed his backpack off the floor and pushed his empty glass towards the landlord. 'And thanks for the drink.'

'Any time.'

***

Will slowed the car and steered it through a gap in the stone wall that separated the church grounds from the lane.

As he applied the handbrake and climbed out, a man appeared at the main door to the eighteenth century building, the familiar white collar of the clergy encircling his neck. He held out his hand as Will approached.

'Will Fletcher? Len phoned to say you were dropping by. I'm Timothy Swift.'

'Thanks for waiting for me.'

The vicar glanced at his watch. 'No problem. I don't have to leave for another twenty minutes. I understand you have a photograph you'd like to show me?'

'I do.'

Will pulled his backpack off his shoulder and reached inside one of the outer pockets. 'I was hoping you could tell me a bit more about him.' He tapped his finger on the man sat at the pub's picnic table. 'Do you know where I can find him?'

The religious man sighed. 'Unfortunately, yes.' He turned away, and then glanced over his shoulder. 'Follow me.'

He led the way round the corner of the church, pushed open a gate to the churchyard, and led Will through carefully tended plots.

The graveyard spread outwards from the back of the church, a muddled collection of stones and tombs jostling for space under the trees that dotted the landscape.

A lone blackbird sang to itself, perched on a moss-laden headstone, then spotted Will and flew away, its scolding tones berating him from a hidden branch.

As he followed, Will's heart sank. With each step farther from the church, the head stones became less moss-covered, and posies of flowers began to appear as epitaphs started to reflect the current century.

The vicar stopped at the end of a row, under a twisted yew tree, then leaned down and pulled away the long grass that had covered the base of the head stone. He crouched down, crossed himself, and then looked up at Will.

'Here he is.'

Will let the breath he'd been holding hiss between his teeth.

Shit.

His eyes skimmed the words on the stone.

Colin Avery, 1961-2013 Friend, ally, soldier of fortune.

'Soldier of fortune?'

'He was a mercenary,' the vicar snapped.

Will jumped at the venom in the man's voice, and waited for him to continue.

The man stood, stretched his back, and leaned a hand on the top of the head stone. 'I managed to glean some information about him from the few friends of his who turned up for his funeral,' he explained. 'His mother used to live in the village – they'd moved over from Northern Ireland in the late nineties. I think he'd been in some sort of trouble.' He frowned, and then shrugged. 'She wouldn't talk about it, and on the few occasions I saw Colin at the pub – never at church, mind – he had a sort of look about him. I was too scared to ask.'

He looked away, embarrassed.

'How did you find out he was a mercenary?'

'It's what got him killed,' said the vicar, slipped his hand into his coat pocket and pulled out a folded piece of paper. 'Here.'

Will took the page, unfolded it and quickly read the photocopied news report.

It seemed life in the village had been too quiet for Avery after his tumultuous youth in Belfast, and he'd disappeared to the Balkans to fight with whoever would pay him the most money.

Will stopped reading, and passed the page back. 'I don't understand – that was over twenty years ago.' His eyes flickered to the death date engraved on the stone. 'It says there he only died a while back.'

'He moved from one conflict to the next,' said the vicar, his disgust apparent. 'Until, one day, his luck ran out – if you can call it that. He decided to go back to his old skill of bomb-making, except the group he was working for got the ingredients mixed up. It blew up in his face.'

The man's gaze fell back to the headstone. 'His poor mother died two weeks after burying her son.' He pointed to the neighbouring stone, then shook his head and began to shuffle back towards the church. 'Such a waste.'

Will took one last glance at the grave, before hurrying after the hunched form of the vicar. 'Why do you think he became a mercenary?'

The man stopped when he reached the gate, and opened it for Will to pass through, before speaking.

'I suppose he just liked killing.'

Chapter 14

'We should've dealt with this twenty years ago,' hissed Gregory. He jabbed a finger at Rossiter. 'I *told* you this would come back to haunt us.'

'Remember who you're talking to,' said Rossiter, his voice menacing as he circled the table towards his press secretary. 'If it wasn't for me, you'd be locked away at Her Majesty's pleasure, not to mention that of the other inmates.'

Gregory flinched at the jibe, and turned his head away so Rossiter wouldn't see the effect his words had on him. It didn't work.

'Yeah. You remember,' said Rossiter. 'You owe me. Don't forget it.'

He stalked past Gregory and moved to the window. The grey sky held a promise of more rain, and he watched, fuming, as a large airliner made its final approach towards Heathrow.

He wondered what his life would be like now, if he'd escaped to the Spanish coastline like so many of his compatriots at the turn of the new century, their ambitions cut short by the politics of peace. Instead, he'd jumped at the opportunity to fill the gap left behind by a northern-based crime syndicate, and obliterated the competition at the same time as his accent.

It had been Gregory's idea for them to attend elocution lessons, of course. A new beginning, new ambitions, a new background history that only the proceeds of crime could pay for.

He snorted. His new identity hadn't even been broken by the UK intelligence services. And here he was, about to embark upon the most audacious plan he and Gregory had devised in their entire working life together.

Rossiter turned and forced his anger into a corner of his mind. Gregory leaned against his desk, his shoulders slumped in the bespoke grey suit that clung so well to his frame.

He'd known Rossiter since they were in their early twenties – both studied at university together, but it was after a particularly raucous drinking session at one of the pubs they frequented during the long winter months in the last year of their studies that Rossiter had shown him the true measure of his ambition.

His words slurred, he'd laid out his plan to complete his degree, worm his way into one of the medium-sized construction companies that was experiencing a boom with the instigation of the recent Peace Accord, and use his influence once there to develop his own business – all within the year.

'But what will you do for capital?' Gregory had frowned over the remnants of his pint. 'No one's going to bankroll a property developer only a year out from his degree.'

Rossiter had waggled a finger at him, a lop-sided grin on his face. He'd leaned forward, nearly toppling off his seat, before clutching the table for balance.

'Drugs,' he'd murmured. 'Lots and lots of drugs.'

He'd giggled like a teenager then, and the pub landlord had weaved through the tables towards them, swiped up their empty glasses and suggested they leave before they got themselves barred.

Rossiter wondered if Gregory could remember the conversation that night. The man in front of him had changed during the subsequent years, to the point where Rossiter felt that none of their alumni brethren would even recognise him now. Maybe one or two, yes – the ones Gregory had purposefully stayed in touch with, should they ever prove useful – but the rest?

He fought down the urge to smile. The rest would probably vote for them, given the way the polls were skyrocketing.

Rossiter flicked his wrists, checked his cufflinks, and then buttoned up his suit jacket. Eventually he spoke.

'I'm sorry, Malcolm,' he said, and cleared his throat. 'You're right. We should've kept looking for it.' He shrugged. 'But we had to get out of Belfast while we still could.'

'I know,' the other man whispered. 'So we deal with it now.' His eyes met Rossiter's. 'Once and for all.'

Rossiter laughed. 'Damned right. I'm not going through this again in another twenty years' time.'

'This isn't the time to be flippant.'

'How do I look?' Rossiter changed the subject, adopting his usual way of deflecting criticism.

'Perfect.' Gregory leaned over the desk and swiped up the loop of material that had been discarded. 'Don't forget your sling.'

Rossiter winked, then tugged the material from his fingers, and placed his over his head. 'Happier now?'

'I'll be happier when you're standing on the threshold of Number Ten waving to the cameras,' said Gregory. He glanced at his watch, a titanium-framed model a former lover had gifted to him. 'We need to go.'

He ushered Rossiter to the door, ran a critical eye over the man's suit, then nodded.

'Right. Let's go and sell this story.'

Chapter 15

Will parked the car next to a television news van, switched off the engine and sat still, listening to the engine tick over as it cooled.

He reached down, unclipped the seat belt, and wondered what the hell he was going to do. He rubbed a hand over his face, then closed his eyes and leaned back against the head-rest, exhausted.

The next minute, a loud banging on the driver's window jerked him awake.

He jumped in his seat, bumped his head against the glass, and opened his eyes to find one of the news team's camera crew grinning at him.

He wound down the window. 'Sorry, I must've dropped off. I'm not blocking you in, am I?'

The man shook his head, re-positioned the weight of the tripod slung across one shoulder and threw a cigarette to the ground, exhaling the smoke over the car roof.

'No, you're all right. Just thought you might want to know the press conference starts in five minutes.'

'Oh, thanks – okay.'

The man nodded, hoisted the tripod farther up his arm, then turned and traipsed towards the house.

Will locked the car and hurried after him, staying a few paces behind.

At the front door, the media representatives were directed by a woman in a black business suit to a room to the left of the door, which opened out into what had at one time been a front reception room.

Will's jaw dropped as he entered the space, which was larger than the floor plan of his and Amy's entire apartment.

'Definitely didn't get this on a politician's wage,' he murmured, as he walked past a long table from where staff served tea and coffee.

He shook his head at the proffered beverages and slid into a seat at the back, next to the door. At the front of the room, a wooden lectern had been erected, a microphone sticking up from its polished beech surface.

Rossiter's election team had been busy, decorating the plain wooden podium so that his trademark coloured banners swung from every available surface.

'Never misses a chance, does he?' grinned a reporter as he slipped into the seat in front of Will. 'Talk about a showman.'

Will mumbled an incoherent response and continued to gaze around the room.

A small public address system comprising two speakers at opposite ends of the room faced outwards, while the sides of the room had been filled with the television cameras of several well-known news outlets.

As the room filled, Will's direct line of sight to the podium became cluttered, and he found that he had to shift in his seat and move his head from side to side if he was going to be able to see Rossiter make his speech.

The general hub-bub of noise dissipated as a door opened, the entrance previously concealed behind one of the wall panels, and Rossiter walked towards the lectern.

He was followed by a slightly shorter man, who wore a grey suit, his salt-and-pepper hair styled fashionably over his skull despite his age, and piercing blue eyes that swept the room, as if gauging the quality of the journalists that had attended.

Rossiter turned to the man, and murmured into his ear. The man nodded, and then Rossiter moved to the microphone and faced the gathered media.

'Ladies and gentlemen, thank you for joining me today,' he said. 'I'll make a brief statement, after which I'll take a few questions. As you'll appreciate, I'm still a little tired from the events of the past twenty-four hours, so please bear with me.'

A polite rumble of voices filled the room, interspersed with the smooth clicks and beeps of digital cameras.

Rossiter cleared his throat, and placed his palm on the one-page statement that had been set on the lectern.

'On Monday, I was returning from an interview with Amy Peters when my car was attacked by masked gunmen. My bodyguard and driver were shot in cold blood, and Miss Peters sustained a bullet wound to her head. Miss Peters remains in a critical condition in hospital. I'd like to thank the staff at the Prince George Hospital for their professionalism and care. Against my doctor's advice, I discharged myself from their care late yesterday afternoon, simply so that their valuable time could be spent looking after patients in more need of their attention than I.'

He pushed the page aside and turned his gaze to his press secretary. Rossiter nodded, and the man glided across the floor to the lectern, cleared his throat, and leaned down to speak into the microphone.

'Ladies and gentlemen, Mr Rossiter will now take questions from the audience.'

Will froze, his heart lurching painfully.

The voice was that of the mysterious caller from yesterday. He was sure of it.

His skin prickled, and he felt a chill across his shoulders as the man continued to field questions and answers from the throng of reporters, before he shifted in his seat to get a better view.

As he peered to the side of the man's head in front of him, he swore under his breath. He now recognised the man from the photograph on Amy's hard drive – he was one of the four men in the first photograph. His hair was flecked through with grey and longer now, but Will was sure it was the same man.

He slumped in his seat, lowering his profile and hoped the man didn't spot him sitting in the audience.

What the hell was going on?

Will realised he'd have to stay out of sight, and then leave the building without the press secretary or Rossiter spotting him. Until he worked through the rest of Amy's notes, he had to assume that the two men were trouble, and meant him harm.

On the other hand, he had to try to find out the man's name. Rossiter hadn't introduced him, and the rest of the press gathered in the room seemed to know who he was.

He cursed, wishing now that he'd taken as much notice of the regular election reporting as Amy had. Instead, he'd tuned it out, tired of the information overload on the television every morning and night.

He turned to the woman to his right, to ask her, but she glanced sideways at him, shook her head and held her phone higher in the air to capture Rossiter's answers as his voice drifted across the room.

Will's mind worked as the questions rumbled around him, Rossiter's calm tones carrying over the murmur of voices in the air.

He glanced to his left, and saw the woman who had chaperoned everyone through the front door now standing in the room, her arms folded, her eyes calmly watching the press conference. Behind her, two men dressed in dark suits wore some sort of communications equipment, the coiled wire to their earpieces curling over their collars.

Will turned his head as the woman next to him raised her hand, and quickly bent down, pretending to tie his shoelace.

The woman caught the press secretary's attention, and jumped to her feet, smartphone raised in the air to record the politician's response.

'Mr Rossiter, have you any idea why your car was targeted and why you were attacked?'

'I'm unable to comment further on the situation, as I'm still assisting the police in every way I can to help them catch the perpetrators of this heinous crime.'

The politician fielded the next two questions from different journalists with a similar response, and then pointed to a man in the front row.

'Yes, Stephen?'

'Do you have a message for the people who attacked you and your staff, Mr Rossiter?'

'Yes. I do,' he said. Rossiter glared at the television camera lens facing him. 'We will catch you,' he said, his tone authoritative. 'And when we do, you will face the full force of the law for the murder of two innocent people and the serious injury of a third.'

'And what of the reporter, Amy Peters, who was shot and wounded? Do you have anything to say to her family?'

Will recognised the speaker as the real reporter from Amy's office, and a colleague of hers that he'd met at the Christmas party. He slouched in his seat to avoid being acknowledged by the man, not wishing Rossiter to know of his presence now, not until he'd figured out what was going on.

'Of course, and please express my gratitude to your editor at this difficult time for his careful reporting of the incident.' Rossiter exhaled, and ran his hand through his hair. 'Sadly, I'm given to believe that Miss Peters has suffered very serious injuries,' he began. 'However, I wish to convey my thoughts to her friends and colleagues and wish her a speedy recovery.'

A relieved expression crossed the politician's face as a different journalist asked for a comment on his election campaign.

'How will the events of the past two days affect your chances of winning the General Election?'

Will watched as a determined expression washed across Rossiter's features.

'They won't,' he said. 'It's business as usual for me.'

He turned to his press secretary and nodded, before moving away from the lectern and striding towards an open door.

'That'll be all the questions today, ladies and gentlemen,' intoned the media expert. 'However, Mr Rossiter appreciates you taking the time to travel to this press conference and would invite you to stay for refreshments in the reception room across the front hall.'

Will wiped his forehead and realised leaving by the front door would be out of the question.

If he was right about the mysterious caller being Rossiter's press secretary, then he could assume that the man knew he was there.

So he had to find another way out of the building.

A house like this would surely have French doors leading from a study, a back door and possibly another door for the hired help, he reasoned. All he had to do was sneak past the security men and get out fast.

As the formalities were concluded, and the press secretary's attention was held fully by the cameras to the right, Will stood and slipped out the room.

The front entranceway was blocked by the two large security men with their backs to him. Nodding to the woman standing just inside the door as he passed, he entered the hallway and waited until her attention was taken by another journalist before he drifted along the passageway, trying door handles and peeking into rooms as he walked.

In the background, the hub-bub of the press conference continued, a white noise to the thoughts rushing around Will's head.

Pushing open an oak-panelled door to his left, he peered round the corner, then stepped over the threshold into what appeared to be a library. By the open patio doors, dust motes danced in the sunbeam that struck the carpet below, while the musty smell of old books filled the air, and he fought the urge to sneeze.

The curtains billowed in the breeze, and he walked farther into the room, mesmerised by the rows and rows of books that lined the shelves.

He ran his fingers over the spines of first editions, antique tomes and yellowed pages.

As he moved around the room, his attention was taken by a group of framed photographs mounted on the wall. He edged closer, peering at each one in turn and realised they represented a visual catalogue of the events that had brought Rossiter and Gregory into the public eye and onto the election campaign.

Will scratched his ear and wondered if Rossiter knew his press secretary had been responsible for his being shot yesterday.

In all of the photographs, the men looked relaxed, smiling, proud of their achievements.

Will didn't get the impression that they had any animosity, and from the news articles relating to Rossiter's rise through the Party's ranks and subsequent polls to date, Malcolm Gregory had almost willingly taken a back seat to ensure the other man's success, but maybe he was having second thoughts and starting to regret that decision.

He froze at movement behind him.

'Who the bloody hell are you?'

Chapter 16

Will turned slowly at the sound of the voice, automatically raising his hands.

The first thought that entered his head was less than polite, but more than appropriate for the moment.

The second was that the woman in front of him was beautiful, even if she was holding a double-barrelled shotgun that was aimed right at his face.

'I said, who the hell are you?'

Will blinked, his gaze fixated on the twin dark pits of the barrels, for a moment wondering if he'd see the double flash that would kill him if the woman's index finger moved.

He risked a glance at her face, and his breath caught.

Dark brown eyes peered out from under a fringe of glossy black hair that tumbled around her face and over her shoulders. She stood a head shorter than Will, the shotgun angled up at his face, the stock held professionally into her shoulder, which was bare under a bright pink vest top. She wore black jeans that moulded to her legs, and stood barefoot on the parquet floor. A silver St Christopher pendant hung around her neck by a delicate chain.

She glared at him along the barrels. 'Have you lost your fucking voice? I asked you a question.'

Will blinked, strangely shocked at the profanity from such a pixie-like figure. Did pixies use guns? He cleared his throat. 'Sorry – I… I couldn't find the toilet so I, um…'

'Thought you'd steal something? You thieving bastard.' The shotgun swung frighteningly closer to his nose.

'No!' Will raised his hands higher. 'Please – I'm not going to hurt you. I'm not a burglar. I was at the press conference – out there.' His mind raced. 'Do you want to see my driver's licence?'

She frowned, the gun jerking away. 'Your driver's licence?'

‘I’ve got a press pass too.’ Will’s gaze traced the line of the barrels as she lowered the gun a little.

‘Show me. Slowly!’

Will kept his left hand raised in the air while his right sought out his wallet in the back pocket of his jeans, his fingers shaking.

He fumbled, dropping the leather case to the floor, and shrugged apologetically.

‘Very fuckin’ funny.’ The shotgun twitched to his face once more. ‘Kick it over here and put your hands on your head.’

Will stepped back as the woman held the gun with one hand and bent down. She flicked his wallet open, pulled out his driver’s licence and held it up. ‘Will Fletcher, eh?’

She stood, removed her finger from the trigger guard of the shotgun, opened the breach, and balanced it in the crook of her arm.

Will’s gaze twitched to the barrels and kept still. The last thing he wanted was to make her even more nervous and give her an excuse to shoot him.

‘Well, I suppose you’d be an idiot of a burglar to be carrying around your driver’s licence.’ Her words interrupted his thoughts and his eyes met hers. A slight crease twitched at her eyes. 'So what the hell are you doing in my uncle's house?'

Will exhaled as she finally lowered the shotgun and removed the cartridges. He dropped his hands from his head, his heart rate slowly returning to some semblance of normal, and cleared his throat.

'I'd heard he was recuperating here,' he began. 'I was hoping he could help me.'

'Help you?' she frowned. 'Does he know you, then?'

Will shook his head. 'He met my girlfriend yesterday morning – before the attack on his car.'

The woman's mouth opened a little, and she raised her eyebrows. 'Amy? The journalist?'

'Yes.'

'Is she okay?'

Will shrugged. 'They tell me it's too early to say.' He looked away, sniffled, and tried to ignore the stinging sensation at the corner of his eyes. He blinked, and then looked back at her. 'Sorry.'

She shook her head. 'No – I'm the one who ought to be apologising. Shit.'

She turned and leaned the shotgun against a small decorative table, made sure it wasn't going to slip, and then glanced back at him. 'You gave me a fright.'

Will's mouth twitched. 'I think we're even.'

She laughed, a gutsy splutter of sound. 'That we are.' She sighed. 'I think we need to start again, Will Fletcher.' She held out her hand. 'Erin Hogarth. I'm Ian Rossiter's niece.'

Will shook her hand, surprised at her firm grip. 'Nice to meet you – I think?'

She laughed again. 'It can only get better, right?' She put her hand on his arm, and then pointed down the hallway behind him. 'Come on. I don't know about you, but after that little scare, I could do with a drink.' She bent down, picked up the shotgun and slung it across her arms. 'I'd better put this back too.'

'Do you actually know how to use it?'

'Of course,' she said over her shoulder. 'How fast can you run?'

Will swallowed, then heard her chuckle under her breath, and shook his head.

She led the way along the hallway, her bare feet soundless on the ornamental rugs that covered the parquet flooring in places.

Will followed mutely, his head turning left and right as he stared at the ostentatious surroundings.

Oil paintings hung on opposing walls, traditional hunting scenes tangling with portraits of humourless men dressed in eighteenth century clothing. Will sensed their unfavourable expressions were frowning down at him.

'Awful, aren't they?' Erin scowled. 'I wish he'd take them down, put something better on the walls.'

'Are they relatives?'

She snorted. 'No. They came with the house. Like everything else around here.' She rapped her knuckles on a mahogany dresser as she passed.

'Listen,' said Will, stopping. 'Would you mind if we got out of here? Maybe go to a pub nearby or something, if you still need that drink?'

'What?'

'I'd rather just leave if you don't mind,' he said. 'I – I really shouldn't have come here. Is there a back door?'

'Back door?' She turned, a confused look on her face.

'Yes. If you don't mind?'

His heartbeat raced. If Erin turned the next corner, he'd be back at the front entrance, facing a minimum of two security guards and one very pissed off press secretary. He had to get out of here and find out what was really going on.

He silently prayed that she wouldn't demand to know why he wanted to avoid the assembled throng at the front of the house, and especially the press secretary – not until he'd fathomed out why the man had threatened him, or what the man's intentions might be in relation to Rossiter.

'We could go for a drink.' The words burst from his lips before he'd had a chance to think.

Erin frowned. 'Um, okay, I guess.'

'Great – my treat, all right?'

'Sure. I'll get my coat and put some shoes on.'

To Will's relief, she turned right, away from the front door and along a passageway that eventually led to a mud room. He watched as she pulled on an old pair of sneakers and shrugged a grey woollen coat over her shoulders.

She opened the back door before turning back to him. 'Come on then, Will Fletcher. I think we need to have a chat anyway.'

Perplexed, Will followed her through the door, and then led the way to his car.

Chapter 17

Ian Rossiter stalked into the room, loosened his tie, then tore the sling from his shoulder and threw it on the desk, oblivious to the opulence of his surroundings.

The press secretary shut the door moments before his employer exploded, then hurried across the floor and waited for the onslaught.

'What the hell is Will Fletcher doing in my house, Gregory?'

'Calm down,' said the other man. 'We don't need the rest of the staff to overhear.' He ran delicate fingers through his thinning grey hair, deliberately keeping his voice low.

Rossiter glared at him, then moved to the window, clasped his hands behind his back and ignored the burning sensation in his shoulder.

'You should keep the sling on. Someone could see you,' said Gregory as he joined him.

'Bugger the sling.'

Rossiter stared through the panels of glass at the motley collection of vehicles strewn across the pristine gravelled turning circle of his driveway, and tried to calm down.

Beyond the driveway, manicured gardens led away from the house, the lawns a lush green after the week's rain. Carefully pruned shrubs and trees dotted the landscape, and he watched as one of the gardeners moved a wheelbarrow across the driveway, cigarette smoke clouding away from him as he walked.

'You didn't answer my question.' He turned away from the window and glared at the press secretary. 'What's Will Fletcher doing here?'

Gregory placed his briefing papers on the desk behind them, and automatically straightened one of the pages that fell loose.

'We didn't know he'd definitely show up,' he began, and held up a hand. 'Let me finish.' He moved around the desk and eased into one of the soft leather armchairs that faced it, and tugged the hem of his trouser leg as he crossed his ankles. 'He's been given a press pass by Kirby Clark. One can only assume the man is trying to help Mr Fletcher.'

'But you approve all the press passes!'

Gregory nodded. 'And I approved his, earlier this morning.'

'Why the hell would you do that?'

The press secretary pointed at the vehicles on the driveway outside. 'Because, right now, one of my security personnel is making sure we know where Mr Fletcher goes.'

Rossiter spun on his heel in time to see a figure stand up and move swiftly away from a blue car parked on the periphery of the driveway.

'Can he be trusted?'

'Absolutely. Been with us for years.'

'What did he do?'

Gregory shrugged, and stared at his fingernails. 'I don't understand the specifics – I don't care to be honest. It's some sort of tracking device.'

'Untraceable?'

'Of course.'

Rossiter turned back to the desk, rolled back his chair and lowered his bulk into the soft material, before leaning forward and unscrewing the cap off a small bottle of pills.

As he shook two into his hand and reached for a glass of water, Gregory frowned.

'How many of those are you taking a day?'

Rossiter tipped back his head, then lowered the glass and re-fastened the bottle cap. 'Don't worry about it.'

Gregory leaned forward. 'I worry, because I need you to be sharper than ever until this is resolved, Ian. Not in some sort of drugged-up haze.'

Rossiter laughed. 'The only thing you worry about is your own future.'

'True. And it's inextricably linked to yours,' said Gregory. 'So, do me a favour and don't fuck it up. We're too close.'

Rossiter reached forward and began to wrap and unwrap the sling around his hands. 'I won't. I told you not to worry about it.' He frowned as another spasm gripped his shoulder muscles, his knuckles turning white as he gripped the desk.

'How bad is it?'

'Bad.'

'He had to do it.'

'I'd have preferred not to have been shot at all.'

'It had to look realistic.'

'Oh, it was realistic all right,' said Rossiter. 'For a moment, I thought he was going to bloody shoot me in the head, too.' He unwrapped the sling, looped it over his head, and shrugged his arm back into it, a pained grimace crossing his features. 'I'll never know how that damned reporter didn't die on the spot like she was supposed to.'

'An unfortunate turn of events.'

'Is she going to die?'

'Too early to tell at the moment, according to the hospital.'

'Can we hurry it along?'

Gregory's face paled. 'Are you serious?'

'It's just a thought.'

'Ian – there's a limit to what we can do here. It's not like the old days.'

'Shame.' Rossiter glanced at his watch. 'What time will the vultures start to leave?'

'In about fifteen minutes. I've instructed Rita to move them on as soon as possible – point out you're recovering and need the peace and quiet.'

'What's next this morning?'

‘A couple of telephone calls, one to that chap in the Midlands who’s keen to lend support to your campaign. He could be a lucrative catch if we can stop him from handing over his money to the bloody Conservatives as usual.’

‘All right. Set it up. I’m taking my niece out to lunch at one o’clock, so make sure we’re done by then.’

‘You should get some rest.’

Rossiter held up his hand. ‘Save it. I’ll rest when this is over and I’m Prime Minister, Malcolm. So will you.’

Chapter 18

Will took his change, then turned and walked back to the armchairs next to the open fire.

Placing the two pints of real ale on the table between them, he sank into the padded material with a sigh, and pushed one of the glasses towards Erin.

'There you go. Apparently it's the local one, and everyone else seems to be drinking it, so it must be good.'

Erin smiled and clinked her glass against his, before taking a sip, and taking an appreciative look at the dark amber liquid. 'That's not bad. I haven't been in here for years.'

They'd driven for twenty minutes after leaving Rossiter's house, the scenery passing the windows in silence. Will wondered if Erin was setting a trap for him, but he was intrigued to know what she wanted to talk about, and so followed her directions.

When she'd instructed him to turn left and the road dipped down into a shady glen, his heartbeat had rocketed, paranoia fuelling the fear that an ambush would take place. He'd sighed aloud when the pub had appeared in view, ignoring the bemused look that had crossed Erin's face.

Will leaned forward and lowered his voice. 'So, what did you want to talk about?'

She glanced across at him. 'You go first.'

'Well, I guess I'd like to know a bit more about your uncle. Seems everything that happened yesterday was because of him, or something he's done.'

'Is that why you came to the press conference?'

'Yes.' Will sighed. 'I'm just trying to make some sense of all this.'

'He's not really my uncle, you know,' said Erin. 'He was a friend of my father's a long time ago. You know Rossiter made his money in construction?'

Will nodded.

'Well, my father used to do some work for him, here and there,' she said. 'So I ended up hanging around building sites in the school holidays, making cups of tea and that sort of stuff.'

'How long since you were last here?' asked Will, easing back into the chair, and resting his pint on the faded green material.

'About a year now.' She shrugged. 'I used to spend holidays down here when I was a kid, before I went away to university at Southampton. Then I moved to London when I graduated.'

'I got the impression back at the house that you know Amy?'

'Yes. I approached her while I was still working in the city a while ago.' Erin caught Will's gaze, then explained. 'I worked for a refugee agency in London since I left university.'

'But not any more?'

She shook her head. 'I needed a break. It's incredibly heart-breaking and frustrating work, in equal measures.'

She took another sip of her pint, and then placed the glass on the table. 'What about you?'

'I work in the archives section at the British Museum.' He glanced down at his hands. 'Doesn't sound very exciting, does it?'

Erin smiled, a wistful expression crossing her face. 'I used to love going to that museum when I was a kid.'

She stopped talking, and turned her gaze to the window.

Will noticed her eyes had turned red, and tears threatened. He leaned forward. 'Hey, is everything all right?'

She nodded, sniffled, and turned back to him. 'Yes. Thanks. It's okay.'

He inhaled the faint scent of her perfume while she regained her composure before speaking again.

'I'd read some of her work last year – remember that article she wrote about the city banker who was skimming off his employers' profits?'

Will nodded, and gestured for her to continue.

'I had some, information, about Rossiter,' she said. 'Information I thought Amy might be able to use.' She held up her hand to stop Will interrupting. 'I'm not prepared to discuss what that was, sorry.'

'Did you stay in touch with her? I mean, after you gave her that information?'

She nodded. 'We probably spoke once a week. I was interested in her progress.'

Will frowned. 'So this story she's been working on – about Rossiter – it was your idea?'

She shook her head. 'She was already researching something about him. I'm not sure what. It was just coincidence that I contacted her at the same time. Gave her another angle to work from.'

Will sank back into his chair and took a sip of his beer, thoughts churning. As he set the glass back on the table, he looked across at Erin.

'Why would you help Amy write a story that could destroy your father's friend?'

'They're not friends any more,' she said. 'Haven't been close for years. They had a falling out a while ago.'

'But you still stay at his house.'

'No – I don't. I just dropped by when I heard he was going to do a press conference from there. I wanted to hear what he said.' She twirled a strand of hair between her fingers as she spoke. 'A bit like you, I suppose. Although I have to say, I didn't expect to see you there.'

'How did you know who I was?'

'Amy told me about you, the first time we met.'

'Did your uncle know you were there?'

'Oh, yes – I phoned ahead. I didn't want to surprise him or anything. He doesn't like surprises.' She broke off and checked her watch and scowled. 'That reminds me. I'm meant to be taking him out to lunch at one o'clock, so you'd better drop me back at the house.'

'Right, okay.'

Confused at the abrupt end to their conversation, Will stood and took the empty pint glasses back to the bar, then followed Erin out the door to the car park.

He unlocked the car, and waited until he started the engine before he spoke again.

'Why are you taking him to lunch?'

She stared at him, and then back to the road as the asphalt passed under the car, the green scenery passing in a blur.

'It's a case of keeping up appearances,' she murmured.

Will didn't know how to respond, so instead he concentrated on his driving, shifted gear and accelerated up the hill.

As they neared the house, Erin held up her hand. 'Stop here.'

Will swung the car over to the left, onto the dirt shoulder of the road, and applied the handbrake.

'Why?'

'Probably not a good idea for you to drive up to the house – in case he sees you.'

'Won't he ask where you've been?'

'I'll tell him I've been out for a walk.'

'Are you going to tell him about me?'

She shook her head. 'I never saw you.'

Will rubbed his hands over his eyes. 'This still doesn't make sense.'

'It will.' She unclipped her seatbelt and let the material slide through her fingers. 'We still have a lot to talk about. Have you got a business card?'

He shook his head.

'So, how do I get hold of you?'

He turned to face her and scrutinised her features.

Could she be trusted?

He sighed, reached over to the glove compartment and pulled out the motel brochure. He turned it over and pointed out the details of the one where he was staying.

'You can ask for me here.'

She took the brochure from him, their fingers touching briefly, and then she folded up the pamphlet and tucked it into the pocket of her jeans.

Opening the passenger door, she turned to him. 'Keep your head down, Will Fletcher. I'll be in touch.'

She slammed the door shut and he watched as she strode up the road and then turned into the driveway of the house.

He sighed, checked his mirrors, then steered a U-turn in the road and headed back to the motel, his mind working overtime.

Somewhere, buried amongst Amy's notes on the hard drive, were some answers.

He hoped.

Chapter 19

Will stared at the computer screen, his mouth slightly open.

As soon as he'd reached the motel, he'd logged on and Googled a search for Rossiter's election team. Under parliamentary law, all of Rossiter's minions had to be listed, together with the roles they undertook during the election period.

Including the man who had presided over the press conference that morning.

On the screen, a headshot of the man in a similarly well-cut suit stared out at him. The professionally-taken photograph had caught the man with his head at a jaunty angle, and a slight smile played across his mouth that didn't quite reach his eyes. He leaned forward towards the photographer, almost as if he was eager to please.

Underneath the photograph, his name was set out in large lettering.

Malcolm Gregory.

Will's eyes skimmed over the biography. It extolled Gregory's previous role as a marketing and communications expert for Rossiter Enterprises, the construction and development company that the ministerial candidate had owned and managed prior to being elected party leader a year previously.

His work history prior to that was potted, glossed over with words such as 'consultant', 'specialist', and 'bespoke services'.

Will shivered, and wondered if those services extended to extortion, burglary and murder.

Did Rossiter know that Gregory was involved in the shooting? Would he know that his media adviser had threatened Will? Did he realise how dangerous the man who was managing his campaign could be?

Will scratched his ear and tried to remember the original quote about keeping one's enemies close, then shook his head, defeated. There was no use in speculating. Whatever the relationship between the man who threatened him and Rossiter, he had to keep digging to find out the truth.

He closed the internet browser and turned his attention instead to the contents of the hard drive.

Now that he had a name for the caller, he wanted to find out whether Amy had stumbled across any information about him other than his official biography. She had a photograph of him with the two men in army fatigues, so surely there must be something else, given the damage that had been done to the apartment.

He stopped, his finger hovering above the mouse button as soon as the realisation hit him.

Gregory must have had Amy followed from work prior to the shooting taking place.

How else would Gregory know where they lived?

He leaned back, reached out for his mug of tea and blew across the hot surface of the liquid.

If Gregory knew where he and Amy lived, what else did he know about them? How long had he been followed?

The landline telephone on the desk emitted a shrill ring, and Will jerked in his seat, sloshing hot tea over his hand.

Cursing, he banged the mug down and reached out to take the call, sucking on the back of his hand to soothe the burning sensation assaulting his skin.

His hand hovered over the receiver, and for a split second he wondered whether he should answer it, before he remembered giving the motel details to Erin, and curiosity won over.

'Will?'

Russell's voice wavered, traffic noise filling the background.

'Hey – what's up?'

'Hang on.'

'Where are you?' Will tucked the phone under his chin, plucked a paper tissue from the complimentary pack on the desk, and dabbed at the tea stains on his jeans. He heard a door slam shut on the other end of the line and waited.

'I'm using the only working public telephone in South-west One. Do you know how rare these things are?'

'Why didn't you phone me from the office?'

'I think we've got a problem.'

Will heard the other man take a shaking breath, and clutched the telephone receiver harder in his hand. 'Russ? Are you okay?'

'Have you checked your email?'

'No – hang on. I'll log in.'

'I sent something to your online account this morning, not your work one.'

'Okay, I'm just taking a look.' Will balanced the receiver under his chin and typed in his login details.

'Have you told anyone that I copied that image file?'

Will stopped typing and gripped the phone. 'No. Why?'

He heard the other man take a shaking breath before he spoke again.

'I think someone is following me.'

Will's insides plummeted. 'Are you sure?'

'Take a look at the photograph I sent you.'

'What's the number there? I'll phone you straight back.'

Will wrote it down, then hung up the phone and dialled the number. Russell answered it before the second ring.

'Okay,' said Will. 'Let me open this file.'

He double-clicked on the image attachment and the new laptop flickered once before the photograph appeared on the screen.

He sucked in his breath.

'You see?' said Russell. 'Now do you realise how much trouble you're in?'

The figure on the left of the four in the now-enhanced picture was Ian Rossiter.

Dressed in plain clothes, he appeared uncomfortable about the photograph being taken, but one of the men has his arm around Rossiter's shoulder, and he seemed to be forcing the faint smile on his face.

A chill ran down Will's spine as the realisation dawned on him. Rossiter had been shot on purpose, to make him look innocent. It could be the only explanation.

'There's more,' said Will.

'What?'

'The original file saved to the hard drive was dated eight months ago. Amy's been pursuing the story for a year now, at least.' Will ran his hand through his hair and began pacing the short space next to the desk, the phone to his ear. He coiled the cord around his fingers as he spoke. 'There must be something else on these files. Otherwise, she could've gone to Rossiter with this photograph ages ago. Yet, she didn't. The photograph alone doesn't prove anything. It just shows him with some people – he could deny all knowledge of knowing them.'

'How much further have you got through the files on that hard drive?'

'About halfway.'

'You need to get a move on,' said his friend. 'I have a feeling you're running out of time.'

'What about you? Are you going to be okay?'

His friend paused before answering. 'I think it might be best if I phone in sick for the rest of this afternoon. I've got somewhere I can stay for a few days.'

'Take the battery out of your mobile, Russ. Just in case.' Will sighed. 'I'm sorry – I really didn't mean to drag you into this. I thought if I came to work rather than phone you, we'd be okay.'

'Just get the bastard, all right? Whatever he's done, or doing – stop him. Before he hurts anyone else.'

'Yeah. Look after yourself. Give me a call tomorrow if you can and I'll give you an update.'

'Got it.'

Will stared at the phone for a moment after his friend disconnected, then placed the receiver back in the cradle.

He sank into the hard chair at the desk and pulled the laptop closer.

In the photograph, Rossiter stood beside the three other men, one being Colin Avery, the other Gregory. The fourth man was still a mystery.

He frowned, then pulled up the Internet search engine and typed in Ian Rossiter's name and the words 'army service'.

Within seconds, several search results appeared on the screen.

As Will scrolled through them, opening the hyperlinks and discounting one name after another, he came to a conclusion.

Rossiter didn't serve in the British Army.

Will scratched his chin and enlarged the photograph on the screen.

If Rossiter wasn't in the army, then what was he doing in a photograph with two men who were dressed in camouflage?

He yawned, checked his watch and was surprised to see the time was past two o'clock in the morning. He leaned forward and began to shut down the computer, flipped shut his notebook and stowed everything into his backpack, before putting the bag next to the bed.

As he lay in the dark waiting for sleep to claim him, he briefly considered going to the police first thing in the morning, before discounting the idea.

Rossiter was too powerful, his press secretary more so, and Will didn't know how far their reach extended.

If he went to the police they might have contacts there, and any chance he had to work out what was going on and how to expose Rossiter would be lost.

And if he pushed too hard, he'd be putting Amy's life at risk. He was sure Rossiter wouldn't be adverse to an attempt on her life, despite the armed guards at the hospital, if he thought his political ambitions were at risk.

He rolled over onto his side, pulling the covers up to his chin as rain lashed the window, the constant hum of the building's air conditioning lulling him to sleep.

He had to keep going, to find enough evidence that Rossiter wouldn't be able to deny anything.

Somehow, in the morning, he had to make progress, before he ran out of time.

Chapter 20

Rossiter hurried along the hallway, then into Gregory's office and slammed the door shut.

'Sir Michael is on board,' he said, rubbing his hands together. 'Not only that, he's arranging an immediate six figure donation – *today*.'

He frowned when Gregory didn't respond with the enthusiasm he'd expect at such news, then realised the man had been sat with his head in his hands since he'd entered the room.

'What is it?'

Gregory raised his head and dropped his hands to the desk, then gestured to his boss to take a seat. 'We have a problem.'

Rossiter felt a pang of worry worm its way around his heart as he lowered himself into the armchair. He folded his arms across his chest. 'What?'

'My people finished working their way through the hard drive last night,' said Gregory. 'Although we've got all of the reporter's notes, they don't include any of the photographs she said she had.'

Rossiter uncrossed his arms and began to tap his fingers on the arm of the chair. 'Nothing at all?'

Gregory shook his head.

'Fuck it.' Rossiter punched the armchair, and then moved until he was standing at the window behind Gregory's chair. 'They're absolutely sure?'

'Yes.'

'What do you plan to do now?'

Gregory turned in his chair and met his boss's stare. 'We've been tracking Will Fletcher since the press conference,' he said, then shrugged. 'We have to assume there's a second copy of the hard drive – one that has everything on it. He may have some original documents too. Including the one we're after.'

He didn't need to mention the exact document to Rossiter. They both knew. They hadn't found it twenty years ago, and although its presence then was dangerous, in light of Rossiter's popularity in pre-election opinion polls, it was becoming even more desperate to find it now.

Neither of the men were inclined to chance speaking about it within the confines of the room, despite Gregory's security team's insistence that the area was swept for listening devices on a daily basis. Closely-run elections often brought out the worst in the competition, and eavesdropping was commonplace. Hell, even Rossiter's team had spies in the other parties.

Rossiter nodded to the patio doors. 'Let's take a walk.'

'Of course,' said Gregory, a false eagerness in his voice. 'I could do with some fresh air after being cooped up in here.'

The two men strolled across the paved patio area that swept around the east wing of the house, then stepped over a low wall and continued their walk along a gravel path that led away from the building. For a moment, the only sound was that of their shoes crunching over the small stones.

Rossiter slowed his pace as they approached a statue set into a fork in the path, then leaned against the base of it, and turned towards the house, gritting his teeth. He beat an uneven rhythm with his clenched fist against the carved stone, the past week's events running through his mind once more as he ran a critical eye over the Georgian mansion that had become his house.

Not a home, he thought. Never that. For the past seven years, he'd been carefully planning, making strategic decisions that would lead, eventually, to the one residential address he'd be more than willing to call home.

Number Ten, Downing Street.

His attention turned back to Gregory and he rubbed his hand over his chin before he finally spoke. 'How do you want to do this?''

'As quietly as possible,' said Gregory.

'How quietly?'

'I think we begin by having him followed, starting now,' said the adviser. 'It's all very well watching his movements electronically, but I'd like a couple of men out there.' He pursed his lips. 'At least then, if anything does need to be done, they're already in position to deal with the matter.'

Rossiter kicked at a large stone. 'Is that wise? Won't there be questions?'

Gregory shook his head. 'They're very good at making it look like suicide or an accident, Ian.'

'Yet you were reluctant to kill the reporter.'

'It's a lot easier to deal with someone who isn't under armed guard,' snapped Gregory.

Rossiter held up his hand. 'You're right, sorry.' He shifted his weight, trying to ease the burning sensation that had started to crawl over his shoulder once more. 'How will we deal with the fallout?'

'All we'd need to do is have you read out a statement at a press conference afterwards conveying your sadness at his passing and suggesting that the shock of his girlfriend being in a coma was obviously too much for him to bear,' said Gregory. 'After that, the media will run with it, the public will accept it, and within twenty-four hours the police will have plenty of other crimes on their hands that will warrant further investigation.' He shrugged, and squinted into the distance.

'The world will have forgotten about Will Fletcher within a week, I guarantee it.'

Chapter 21

Will caught movement out the corner of his eye, lowered the newspaper he was reading, and then stood as Erin Hogarth approached his table in the motel's small restaurant.

'Good morning,' he said, pulling out a chair for her.

She acknowledged the gesture with a small smile. 'Morning.'

As Will returned to his seat, a waitress appeared. 'The kitchen closes in ten minutes,' she said. 'What can I get for you?'

She handed a menu to Erin, and then thrust an identical one under Will's nose. 'There's no more grapefruit juice,' she said.

Will ignored her and turned his attention to Erin. 'Have you eaten this morning?'

'Not yet.' She closed the menu and handed it back to the waitress. 'I'll have a black coffee and the poached eggs on toast, please.'

The waitress arched an eyebrow at Will.

'Full English,' he said. 'And coffee.'

When the waitress had retreated to the kitchen, he propped his elbows on the table.

'Why did you want to see me so urgently?' he asked. 'I was surprised to hear from you so soon.'

Erin played with her paper napkin. 'I hope I didn't wake you up.' She screwed the napkin into a ball. 'I didn't realise it was so early until after I put the phone down.'

Will shrugged. 'It doesn't matter. What did you want to talk about?'

Her gaze shifted, and the waitress reappeared.

They waited while she deposited a coffee pot, milk and sugar, and then walked away once more.

Erin leaned forward and lowered her voice.

'There were some people at the house last night,' she said. 'People I haven't seen before.'

She picked up the coffee pot and filled both their cups.

Will frowned. 'Your uncle – sorry, Rossiter – is trying to win a General Election,' he said. 'I'm sure there are a few people you haven't seen around before. He must be pulling in everyone he knows to help him win the election.'

She shook her head. 'No – they weren't like the usual people.'

'What do you mean?'

She reached across and tore open a sugar packet, stirring the contents into her coffee. 'These people arrived just after it got dark. They weren't wearing suits, or anything else that you'd expect a campaign team to wear.' She put the spoon down. 'I don't know, Will – two men turn up late at night, with equipment cases, and disappear into a room that Gregory has cordoned off so no one can enter it without his permission. What does that tell you?'

'Rossiter, or Gregory, didn't want the rest of the campaign team to know what they were doing there?'

'Exactly.'

The aroma of fried food reached Will's senses moments before the waitress reappeared with their breakfasts, and they stopped talking while they attacked the food.

After a few moments, once Will's stomach had stopped rumbling, he set down his knife and fork and took a sip of coffee.

'I wonder what they were doing there.'

Erin shook her head. 'I've got no idea. I wasn't staying at the house so it would have seemed odd if I'd hung around any longer. I saw Gregory go into the room after they arrived – he was only with them for fifteen minutes or so, and then went back to his own office.'

'Did Rossiter say anything to you before you left?' Will dug his fork into a piece of bacon, relishing the greasy taste as it hit his taste buds.

'No. I wandered into his study to let him know I was leaving. He seemed distracted, but had a heap of campaign press releases on his desk so I figured he was concentrating on those.'

She pushed her plate away and sighed. 'I needed that, thanks.'

Will finished his breakfast and topped up their coffee. 'Do you think they were there because of what Amy was working on?'

'I do, yes.'

'Do you know what else she was investigating? I mean, before you contacted her?'

Erin shook her head, her brow creasing. 'She wouldn't say – and I don't think she was being secretive on purpose,' she said, holding up a hand to stop Will's protest. 'She was doing her job – making sure she had all the facts right – before she made anything public. Cross-checking everything, you know?'

Will nodded. It sounded exactly the way Amy worked.

'I know it was something to do with his past,' Erin mused. 'Something to do with how his construction business had been set up in the first place.'

'What's the connection with your father?' asked Will. 'How do they know each other?'

'I'm not sure,' said Erin. 'I lived with my mum until I was seven. Dad reappeared one day and moved back in.' She looked away. 'Mum died in a road accident six months later.'

Will reached across and squeezed her hand. 'I'm sorry.'

'Thank you.' She cleared her throat. 'Not long after that, Dad got a phone call from Ian, offering him some work down this way, and we moved south.'

'Do you know where your Dad had been?'

'Northern Ireland.'

Will let his gaze wander round the empty restaurant. 'So, your father and your uncle worked together over in Belfast, is that what you're saying?'

'Yes. Dad always worked in construction – he was an electrician. I think that's how they met when they were younger.'

Will tapped his bottom lip. 'But Rossiter didn't start his construction business until 2000 here,' he murmured. 'So how did they know each other in Belfast if Rossiter wasn't running a construction business at that time?'

Erin shrugged, and then frowned. 'I'm not sure. Maybe that's the angle Amy has been investigating?'

Will opened his mouth to tell her about the hard drive, before he clamped it shut. He still didn't know whether he could trust Erin and, at the moment, there were some thoughts he wanted to keep to himself – at least until he'd had a chance to finish going through

Amy's files. He leaned forward and rubbed his hand over his face before balancing his elbows on his knees.

'What are you thinking?' said Erin.

He shrugged. 'I'm wondering what to do next.'

'You might want to go and talk to your mother.'

Will sat up straight. 'What? What would make you say that? How do you know my mother?'

'I don't,' said Erin. 'But the last time I saw Amy, she mentioned that she was going to go and see her.'

'When was this?'

'About a month ago. We caught up for a coffee when I was in the city for a meeting.' She sighed. 'I was getting scared. I wanted to know what she was doing about Rossiter. I wanted to know whether she'd confronted him with what I'd told her.'

When Will raised an eyebrow at her, she shrugged. 'She hadn't – she was still collecting evidence for the main angle of her story. And she wasn't telling anyone anything that would mean her losing her advantage, either. She wasn't going to let anyone else near this story.'

Will slumped back into the folds of the chair.

'She didn't tell you she went to see her, did she?' Erin picked up her coffee and stared at him over the rim of the cup, before taking a sip.

Will sighed. 'No. No, she didn't.'

Chapter 22

Will rubbed his hands over his face, and pushed the chair back from the small desk. He'd gone back to the room after Erin had left, the echoes of their conversation filling his mind.

He'd decided to spend the rest of the morning completing his search through Amy's files and notes before doing anything else.

He'd gone round in circles, trying to find anything that would lead to a clue about Rossiter's university days, but the search engine results were noticeably thin.

Someone had ensured that the man's background information didn't include whatever he'd done in Northern Ireland, or once he'd first arrived back in England.

Will groaned. It would have been incredibly easy to erase any unsavoury history before the internet search engine had really taken off, and that was exactly what someone had done.

He leaned over and picked up the mug of tea next to the laptop, then grimaced as he took a sip and remembered it was an hour old.

He realised he had to catch up with where Amy had got to in her investigation – and fast.

Too many gaps in his knowledge were beginning to show, evidenced by Erin's knowledge of Amy's visit to his mother.

And the fact that Amy hadn't told him about the visit.

***

The low-set brick clad building formed an L-shape around the asphalt driveway, the space outside its front doors accompanied by signs demarking their use by ambulances only.

Will had parked in a space in the visitor's car park, then had walked the length of the building, signed in at reception and now tried to ignore the fact that his backside was turning numb in the hard plastic chair he'd been directed to.

The facility manager had frowned at his calling in without phoning ahead.

'It upsets her routine,' she'd grumbled.

Will had apologised, and asked to meet with his mother in her private room, away from the prying eyes and ears of the facility's staff and more alert residents.

She'd huffed, but said she'd go and see if his mother was awake and comfortable, then turned her back on him and stalked away.

Twenty minutes later she reappeared, beckoned to him to join her, and led him to his mother's room before closing the door behind him.

He pulled a chair over to where his mother sat, her white hair haloed by the sunshine pouring through the window, the panes smeared from the recent rainfall.

She played with a loose thread on the blanket across her legs, and smiled at him as he joined her.

'How're you doing, mum?'

He tried to recall when he'd last been to see her, the guilt coursing through him as he realised it had been months, rather than weeks.

'It's good to see you,' she murmured. 'I know you're busy, but I worry you work too hard.'

Will lowered his gaze to his hands and shuffled in his seat, trying to get comfortable. 'Amy's in hospital, mum.'

Her hand found his, and she squeezed. 'Is it bad?'

He nodded, fighting back tears. 'She was injured. Badly.' He sniffled. 'I still don't know if she's going to be okay.'

He exhaled as his mother squeezed his hand, then her fingers returned to the blanket, pulling the thread.

He wondered how much she was listening, how much she was taking in, whether her damaged brain was working through what he'd told her.

'It was so nice of her to visit.'

'When?'

She waved her hand. 'Oh, I don't know. You know how it is with me and time.'

'Well, how about a guess? A few weeks? A month?'

His mother turned her face towards the window, her features devoid of expression. She seemed to be watching a pair of sparrows frolicking in a bird bath in the middle of the threadbare lawn, her eyes flickering back and forth.

Will clenched his fingers into his palms and forced down his impatience. He knew how this worked. Sometimes his mother would retreat into her own thoughts for minutes, days even, and it did no good to try to hurry her along.

He followed her gaze to the bird bath, just in time to see a large pigeon dive-bomb into the water, sending the smaller birds scattering in its wake.

His mother giggled, then turned to him. 'Oh, it was only a couple of weeks ago – I remember now.'

'Why?' He paused. 'I mean – why did she come to see you, without me?'

His mother shrugged, a blissful smile on her lips. 'She didn't say.'

'What did she want?'

'I-I don't remember.'

'Can you try?'

'Mmm.'

Will exhaled, forced his frustration down deep, and waited. When it was apparent his mother wouldn't volunteer any more information without being prompted, he tried a different tact.

'What was she wearing?'

His mother laughed again, a beautiful sound that filled the room.

Will tried desperately to keep his emotions in check. It had been so rarely that he'd heard his mother laugh freely.

His mother was still giggling when she spoke again. 'She was wearing an awful old cardigan – goodness knows where she'd found it. It was much too long for her,' she said. 'And a hat – a big floppy one that hung over her ears.'

Will's mind raced. The only reason he could think of why Amy would wear such strange clothing was that she had disguised herself to visit his mother, which meant she was already fearful for her life, and concerned that she was being followed by someone.

'And she was wearing sunglasses,' added his mother, a wide smile on her face, the giggles subsiding. 'It was raining outside, I remember – and she was wearing sunglasses. I told her she should have brought an umbrella instead.'

She fell silent, and her gaze dropped back to the blanket. She tugged hard at the thread and it came loose.

'Can you remember what she came here for?' asked Will.

His mother twisted the thread around her index finger, her mouth downturned. She sniffled.

'I can't remember,' she whispered.

'Come on, mum,' he urged. 'Please.'

He slid off his chair and knelt on the floor by her side, took her hand in his once more, and prised her fingers away from the threads she had tugged from the blanket.

Her skin felt cool to his touch, smooth and comforting. He screwed his eyes shut against the memories that threatened tears, pushed the thought aside, then looked at her.

'I need your help, mum. So does Amy,' he said. 'The smallest thing – it doesn't matter if you don't think it's important.'

He squeezed her hand, and then sat on his heels. His heart raced. If he pushed too hard, her mind would close down, block him out and he'd lose her again. But if she could remember…

'The bible,' his mother said, a smile lighting up her face. 'She wanted my bible.' Her gaze turned to him, her eyes shining. 'I remembered!'

'You did, mum – you did great.' Will stood, then leaned down and hugged her. 'Did she say why she wanted it?' he asked, returning to his chair.

He couldn't understand why his mother would let her most treasured possession out of her sight, let alone give it to Amy. He held his breath as he watched his mother's mouth work, a frown creasing her brow, and opened his mouth to speak.

She held up a finger, before shaking her head. 'Shh, Will. Don't rush me.'

He leaned forwards, his elbows on his knees, holding his breath.

A smile lit up his mother's face. 'That was it! She said she was going to put it somewhere safe!'

Somewhere safe?

Will turned over the phrase in his mind.

Why? What was so important about his mother's old bible?

Was that why the apartment had been broken into?

He tugged at his earlobe. ‘I don’t suppose she told you where she was going to put it?’

His mother shrugged. ‘She said she was going to put it back where it belonged.’

Will sighed. ‘It couldn’t be simple, could it?’

Chapter 23

Later, after he'd said his goodbyes and checked in on the facility manager to make sure his mother was otherwise okay, Will stomped back to the car, lost in thought.

Somewhere safe. Back where it belonged.

Not the apartment, he mused. Amy must've known that Rossiter would have no qualms about paying someone to break in and tear the place apart to search for the bible – if that's what he was after.

Not the newspaper offices, either. Notwithstanding the fact Amy hadn't told him or Erin about the angle of her story, she wouldn't risk one of her colleagues beating her to it.

And there had been nothing else in their shared post office box, or saved to the hard drive.

He groaned, and then banged his hands on the steering wheel in frustration. What if Amy had a second, private, post office box which she hadn't told him about?

He shook his head to clear the thought. No – everything Amy had left for him so far had been similar to a trail of breadcrumbs. She was leading him to the story – he just had to figure it out.

Before Rossiter found him.

Before the whole story was covered up.

He emitted a growl of frustration, then started the car and drove away from the aged care facility, switching on the radio in time to catch the hourly headlines.

While the radio announcer intoned that day's news, he realised he was running out of time.

The General Election was only a week away. And Rossiter wanted to win.

Badly.

At any cost.

Will glanced at his backpack on the passenger seat, the hard drive and his laptop safely tucked inside.

What the hell am I missing?

What aren't I seeing?

And where the hell is that bible?

***

Will's eyelids snapped open, his heart racing.

He squinted at the luminous dial of his wristwatch, then rolled over, reached out his hand and switched on the bedside lamp.

Three-thirty a.m.

He rubbed his eyes and desperately tried to recall the thought that had shaken him from his sleep.

In his dream, he'd been running after Amy, unable to catch up with her. Paper copies of her notes fluttered in his hands as he'd gasped for oxygen to feed his tired muscles.

In front, Amy raced through long grass, tossing more pages into the air. She had glanced over her shoulder at him, laughing. 'Keep up Will – we're almost there!'

He'd tripped then, and all the paper he held had flown up into the air, before floating to the ground. He'd stood, brushing dirt off his jeans, and had held out his hands as the large confetti fell around him, and then realised they were standing in a graveyard.

At which point, he'd woken.

Will swung his legs over the bed and padded into the bathroom for a glass of water.

Twisting the faucet, he glanced up at his reflection in the mirror, playing over the end of the dream in his mind. He shook his head in frustration, turned off the tap and took a deep gulp of the cool water.

And nearly choked.

His hand shaking, he placed the glass on the counter and tried to calm his jangled nerves.

That was it. The safe place.

Bibles belonged in churches.

Amy had put the bible in the church.

The one where Colin Avery was buried.

Will dashed back to the bedroom and switched on the laptop. He began to pull on his clothes as he waited for the computer to start up, then sank into the chair and began to sort through the files on the hard drive.

Somewhere, in one of the files, Amy had confirmed his suspicions and left him a clue, he was sure.

He just had to find it.

***

Will parked the car behind the Green Dragon pub and followed the faded signs for the church to a wooden stile built into a fence that straddled a meadow. A footpath led through the field, skirting a small copse of trees to the left. The church had its own parking area, but the opportunity to stretch his legs while he worked through what he had learned was tempting. So too was the thought of a quick pint at the pub on his return.

He'd stopped at a service station half a mile down the road from the motel, pausing only to buy a stale heated meat pie and an energy drink.

A truck driver had grinned at him as they waited in the queue at the counter and pointed at Will's purchases.

'Food of kings,' he'd said.

Will had taken one look at the man's large physique, wondered how long he had before having a heart attack, and smiled politely before handing over his money to the cashier and exiting the shop as quickly as possible.

Now, the hem of his jeans tugged at the long grass as he walked, and he kept a wary eye on the small herd of cows huddled near a stream that ran through the lower part of the meadow.

He couldn't make up his mind about Rossiter's niece. Was she really trying to destroy her uncle's career, or was Rossiter using her to track his movements?

Why had she contacted Amy? What had made her turn against her father's old friend?

He scowled and thrust his fists deeper into his pockets, his nails scratching his palms. Only three days ago, life had been near-perfect and the biggest worry he'd had was whether Russell was going to kick his arse at their next fencing match.

He sniffled, battled the stinging sensation behind his eyelids and stomped along the path.

It narrowed as it reached the trees, and the grass fell away to reveal a pale coloured mud, with puddles several inches deep in places. Branches hung over the footpath, creating a green tunnel pockmarked with blackberry bushes and rosehip brambles.

Will stopped and turned. A mile back, the thatched roof of the pub poked above the hedgerow that surrounded its boundary line. A crow cawed as it banked gently on the air, before it sank to the meadow with an effortless grace.

No one followed.

Will exhaled, only then realising that he'd been holding his breath, waiting. His heart raced, but he wasn't sure if that was from the undulating walk across the field, or the fact that he was scared.

Very scared.

He wished Amy had told him more about the story that had been her obsession for the past few months. Maybe he could have suggested a way that she could pursue the political candidate without putting herself in danger.

He was out of his depth, and all too aware of it.

Here he was, chasing after clues Amy had left behind, on the trail of the same investigation that had surely led to her being shot.

He ignored the stinging sensation that pricked his eyes, loneliness washing over him, leaving him desolate.

He wished he could pick up the phone, call the police detective and tell him everything, but his conscience couldn't let go of the fact that he simply didn't have enough proof.

Of course, the police would carry out their own enquiries, but by the time they came to any useful conclusions, it would be too late.

Rossiter would, in all likelihood, be Prime Minister and he and Malcolm Gregory would create a smokescreen so complex that he and Amy would spend the rest of their lives looking over their shoulders.

If they lived that long.

He spun on his heel and continued towards the church. The sign by the stile had said it was only one and a half miles, and his pace increased. He pulled his hands from his pockets and swung his arms at his side, eager to test his theory.

If he'd interpreted his mother's cryptic words about Amy's visit, he was on the right track. If not –

A branch snapped in the woodland to his left. He froze.

Straining his ears, he tried to listen beyond the cacophony of crows that rose from the trees above him, wheeling and rising into the air in fright.

He cried out in terror as a blackbird tore from the brambles next to him, before steadying himself, and then fell silent as a small deer emerged from the woodland.

He held his breath, mesmerised by the sight of something moving with such precision and grace, and watched as she raised her head, twitched her ears, and then bounded across the meadow towards the stream and the safety of the copse of trees below.

He smiled, berated himself for reacting so badly, and continued his way along the path.

He'd never spent a lot of time in the countryside. He'd played in a park near his house as a kid, but the novelty of tearing around an enclosed green space at a weekend had worn off as he'd entered his teenage years and instead he'd been more comfortable amongst the concrete and brick buildings of cities.

He began to take more notice of his surroundings, enjoying the fresh air and sense of freedom that came from being outside – *really* outside – and began to make plans to bring Amy out of the city more often.

Then he frowned, as he remembered she'd already been here. Without him.

As the trees led the footpath round a left-hand curve, the church steeple appeared, rising majestically above a horizon of oak and yew trees. A second stile marked the boundary of the field and as he climbed over, he was relieved to see the footpath change from mud to gravel, which crunched under his feet.

The path widened and as he turned a corner and walked under the shadow of the eighteenth century building, he noted the empty visitor car parking spaces to the right of the door.

There was no sign of the vicar's car in its allocated space.

He remembered as a child that churches were often left unlocked so that penitent parishioners and visitors could come and go as they pleased, but wondered if the vandalism of the twenty-first century had caught up with tradition and would dictate otherwise.

He raised his hand and pushed against the old wooden surface, and was relieved when it swung inwards under his touch.

He entered a small porch with wooden benches either side, coloured paper notices for garden parties, fund-raisers and community events fluttering in the breeze from the open door. The papers fell silent as he pushed the door shut, and then made his way through to the nave.

The building opened out into a large space, with vaulted ceilings towering above the stone slab floor. Dust motes drifted in the air between the stained glass windows. Light filtered through the coloured panes, pools of light breaking up the gloom as he wandered across the large flagstone floor.

Will closed his eyes and inhaled the musty air, childhood memories flooding into his mind. A hush filled the room, cocooning him from the outside world. He opened his eyes, sneezed twice, and then turned towards the altar at the far right of the church.

He approached the front pew to the left of the altar, running his hand over the polished wooden surface.

Small posies of flowers adorned the outside of the pew facing the aisle, hanging in wire mesh display sconces. Prayer cushions were neatly propped up behind the front of each pew, their covers displaying the colours and emblems of the local Girl Guides, Women's Institute and every other community group that had banded together to weave the tapestry covers.

Finally, in front of each place and without regard to any dwindling size of the congregation, a bible lay.

The brown mock-leather covers held a dull sheen in the subdued light, and Will realised Amy had recognised the books as being similar in style to his mother's bible. He sighed, and began to methodically work his way to the back of the church, craning his neck as he passed each pew, occasionally shuffling his way down a pew to inspect an opened book, before returning to his search.

He growled in frustration as he reached the back of the church, crossed the nave, and resumed his search from the back of the right-hand row.

He stopped halfway, the need to stretch his neck from the strange angle he'd been holding it at slowing him for a moment. He breathed out, and gazed across the room to the vestry, and the stairs beyond it that led up towards a balcony, and more pews.

Will thought twice about cursing, lowered his gaze and returned to the task in hand. As he progressed from the row back towards the altar, he realised if he didn't find his mother's bible here, he'd have no idea where to look next. Amy's research and the way she'd catalogued the details, were filed in such a way, it could take him days to find out what she'd discovered.

He approached the penultimate pew, resigned to the fact that he'd have to start on the balcony next, when something caught his eye. He back-tracked until he was level with the pew again.

His heart twitched excitedly, and he forced the sensation aside. He slid onto the pew, grateful for the excuse to sit for a moment, and then reached out for the book.

As his palms slid over the smooth surface, memories engulfed him.

His mother reaching to her sewing table on a Sunday, picking up the bible to return to the dining table, insistent that her children pray before eating their lunch.

Or the times she quietly read the book while his father watched the six o'clock news in the evening, finding comfort between the pages as the world's troubles filled the screen.

He blinked, pulled the book towards him, and tucked it into the inside of his jacket.

A car's engine roared outside, jerking him back to the present.

He rose from the pew, the crunch of gravel beneath tyres unmistakable.

He swallowed, the hair on the back of his neck standing on end, while goose bumps prickled his skin.

Will moved, fast. He jogged towards the back of the church, deciding that regardless of whose car had turned up, he wasn't going to hang around to introduce himself.

He pushed through the door to the vestry, closed it behind him and ran to the plain window set high in the wall. Standing on tiptoe, he peered through a yellowed net curtain to the car park.

Outside, an old silver sedan had stopped outside the porch, and two men were climbing out.

The driver wore a three-quarter length black wool coat, his greying hair swept back off his face. He squinted as he peered up at the church spire, then lowered his gaze to turn to the passenger who was leaning on the car roof, his hands folded, a quizzical expression crossing his brow.

The man's mouth moved, but the words were lost to Will as he held his breath, waiting, unsure what to do.

Then, the car doors slammed, and the driver flicked his coat off his hip, turned, and extracted a gun before walking to the front door of the church, closely followed by his accomplice.

Will emitted a small yelp, and quickly assessed his surroundings. He needed to get away – quickly, before the two men discovered him, and the bible.

The room was full of detritus – props from a past Nativity play jostled for space with stocks of candles, flower arranging tools and chairs stacked against one wall.

Will spun in the centre of the vestry, his mind racing.

The front door to the church slammed shut with a loud crash, and the men's footsteps reverberated across the flagstones as they began to prowl.

'Come on, come on,' muttered Will as he raced towards one of the doors in the opposite wall, carefully threading between the paraphernalia cluttering the way.

He wrenched open the first door, ready to run out of the building and away to his car, then swore.

He'd discovered a wardrobe instead.

Chapter 24

Will hurried from the back of the church, having finally found the right door, and slipped out the vestry.

He ignored the woman leaving the churchyard with her black Labrador in tow, a shocked expression crossing her face as he picked up his pace and tore past her, the white and black robes of the parish rector billowing from his shoulders.

He charged across the car park and round the back of the building, the stolen robes flapping behind him, his footsteps spraying gravel across the paintwork of the stationary car in front of the porch.

Will cleared the stile in one swift movement, and ran, expecting a shout closely followed by two men with guns at any time.

As he rounded the corner, the footpath began its steady drop towards the village pub, and he slid to a stop.

Tearing the vicar's robes from his shoulders, he bundled them together, bent down and pushed the material into the back of the blackberry bushes.

Extracting his arms carefully from the brambles, he leaned forward and put his hands on his knees, panting.

He grabbed the front of his jacket, suddenly paranoid that he'd dropped his mother's bible, and nearly cried with relief when he felt its familiar surface.

He gulped in more air, and then began to hurry across the meadow towards the safety of the pub and his car.

How the hell had they found him? And so quickly?

He chewed his bottom lip as he panted his way down the last part of the footpath.

Either Amy had left more information on the first hard drive than he'd thought, or –

He frowned. Or Rossiter's niece had told them where to find him.

Anger flushed through him, swiftly replaced by guilt. Had she volunteered the information, or had something happened to her since he'd left the motel that morning?

He hadn't heard from her since they'd had breakfast.

Was she okay?

His pace quickened, and he jogged the last few steps. He climbed the wooden stile that led to the asphalt-topped car park and noted that the pub had filled considerably in the time he'd been at the church. He checked his watch and realised it was fast approaching lunchtime.

He glanced over his shoulder, expecting to see two shadowy figures on the footpath farther up the field, but it was deserted. He pulled the car keys from his pocket and hurried towards the vehicle, and had hit the remote locking switch when he heard it.

A car engine, still some distance away, roaring through the lanes, and coming closer.

He cursed, paranoia sweeping over him. He slid into the driver's seat and slammed the door, gunned the engine – and stalled it.

Swearing, he wiped the sweat running down his forehead, reset the gears to neutral, and re-started the car. This time, he forced himself to ease off the clutch, slid the car into first gear, and then turned towards the exit.

He wound down the windows, leaned forward and switched off the radio.

Sure enough, the now-familiar growl of the silver sedan was drawing closer, changing gears as it powered down the hill towards the pub.

Will realised it would be seconds before it turned the corner and caught up with him, and quickly swung the car to the left.

The vehicle bucked as he forced it into third gear, Russell's warning remembered too late. Will kept his foot on the throttle and powered back to second, the engine revving in protest.

He sped round a right-handed turn, saw the national speed limit sign at the exit of the village boundary, and jumped the car straight into fourth.

He checked the rear-view mirror.

No silver car.

He breathed out. His ruse had worked. Hopefully, whoever was looking for him would waste precious minutes checking the pub for any trace of him.

He wiped a trickle of sweat from his brow as his thoughts returned to Rossiter's niece.

He'd have to return to the motel to collect his clothes, but after that, what?

What if she was innocent? What if she was telling the truth about Rossiter?

What if she was lying?

***

It took Will three attempts at swiping his motel card before the door to his room unlocked with a smooth *click*.

Cursing his shaking hands, he shrugged off his jacket and pulled out the laptop and hard drive from his backpack.

He wondered, without hope, whether Amy had left a clue as to the importance of the bible in her notes. He couldn't recall seeing anything the first time he'd read through them, but as he came to learn more about her investigation into Rossiter's activities, he began to notice things he'd previously missed.

Yet he still didn't have enough, in his view, to justify Rossiter's actions to date, which resembled that of a desperate man.

A desperate man is a dangerous man. Hadn't he once heard his father quote that line?

He wracked his memory trying to remember where the quote came from as he waited for the computer to go through its start-up sequence.

As soon as it was ready, he pulled out a chair and sat heavily, glancing up at the failing light outside.

He frowned at the dark clouds forming, then stood and pulled the curtains closed, switching on the desk lamp on his return to his seat.

Despite taking the precaution of pulling apart his mobile phone, he couldn't shake the feeling of being watched. He realised it was paranoia, caused in part by what he was reading in Amy's notes, but also by the actions of the armed men in the silver sedan earlier that day, and finding out who the mysterious caller was.

He congratulated himself on his quick thinking that afternoon, and the fact that he'd outwitted them, and settled in to read through the files on the hard drive once more.

Rain began to beat against the windows, lashed onto the glass by gusts of wind, and Will absently reached across and flicked the wall heater on, before returning to the screen, lost in his reading.

A loud knock on the door made him freeze, his fingers hovering over the keyboard.

Chapter 25

Will searched the room for something, anything, he could use as a weapon.

He pulled open the wardrobe, and found a broken umbrella shoved into a back corner, missed by an errant cleaner. Snatching it, he turned back to the door at another knock, louder this time – more insistent.

He hurried across to the desk and stuffed the laptop and hard drive into his backpack, not waiting for the system to shut down. Kicking the backpack under the bed, he moved to the door.

His hand hovered over the chain mechanism, before he cursed.

When he checked into the room, he never thought to find out if he could open the door with the chain still attached. As it was, the door took up the whole end of a short passageway rather than opening out into the room, so he couldn't open the door to see who was outside without removing the chain – there simply wasn't enough room to crane his head around the door to look.

'Shit,' he muttered, hefted the makeshift weapon in his right hand, and wiggled the chain from its fixing.

He grabbed the door handle, twisted it, and swung the door open, weapon raised.

His mouth dropped open in shock.

Erin stood in the hallway, hair plastered to her head, her clothing soaked through. Mascara ran down her face, a bruise covered one cheek, and she hugged her arms to her chest, shivering.

'Let me in,' she said through chattering teeth. 'Quickly.'

Will stood aside, let her pass, then slammed the door shut and re-locked it. He propped the umbrella against the doorframe before turning to her.

She was moving fast through the apartment, grabbing Will's things and shoving them into his hands.

'What's going on, Erin?'

'We need to move – now.'

'Why?'

'He's found you.'

'Rossiter?'

'And his cronies.' She threw his jacket at him. 'They came here earlier. I saw them.'

She stopped, dead centre in the middle of the room, and dropped his jacket on the floor.

Only then did he realise her hands were shaking, an uncontrollable tremor that couldn't be explained away by the cold rain she'd obviously been standing in.

'What happened to your face?' he asked, dropping his belongings onto the bed and pulling out the backpack from under it.

'He found out I'd spoken to you,' she said. 'I said I'd met you at the press conference, and that you'd offered to buy me a drink, that's all.' She sniffled, and turned away. 'He hit me anyway.'

In two strides, he covered the space between them, and instinctively drew her into his arms.

'It's okay, we'll move,' he soothed. His gaze wandered the room as he spoke. Some toiletries in the bathroom – a razor, toothpaste – and he'd be clear. 'I'll grab the rest of my stuff. Go out to the car and wait for me, we'll find another motel.'

She pulled away, shaking her head. 'Don't you get it?' Her voice rose. 'How the hell do you think they found you?'

'What do you mean? I haven't used my phone since I've been here – the battery's out of it, look!' He pointed at the separated parts on the bedside table. 'So, unless someone told them where to find me…'

'What – you're accusing me now?' she sneered. 'Bloody hell, Will – give me some credit!'

'Well, what do you expect? I only met you two days ago – I tell you where I'm staying, and then suddenly your uncle and his henchmen track me down!'

Erin's eyes narrowed, and she folded her arms across her chest. 'This all kicked off between you and my uncle before you even met me, Will, so don't you *dare* accuse me of being a traitor.'

'There's no other explanation!' He watched as she took a deep breath.

'When we spoke yesterday, you said your apartment had been trashed and you'd been getting instructions from an unknown caller, yes?'

He nodded.

'Have you heard from him since you dropped off the hard drive on Monday, even though by now he's probably realised you haven't run to the police and that you're *somehow* still going after Rossiter?'

'No.' He bit his lip.

She took a step back. 'You know who the caller is, don't you?

He nodded. 'It's Malcolm Gregory.'

Her face paled. 'Are you sure?'

He shrugged. 'Yes.' He bent down and picked up a sock that had been missed in their frantic rush through the motel room, and tucked it into his backpack. 'Maybe I haven't heard from him because he's still going through the files?'

She shot him a look of disbelief, uncrossed her arms and huffed in frustration. 'Will – think! The only reason why he wouldn't be phoning you now is that he doesn't *need* to. So, what does that tell you?'

Will's insides plummeted. 'He's following me,' he mumbled. 'How?'

'They traced your car! They've probably realised you'll avoid the phone!'

Will swallowed, the reality of Erin's words hitting him hard.

'How?'

She shrugged. 'I don't know – either Rossiter's got someone on his payroll who can access the CCTV network and they've traced your licence plate, or,' she shivered again, 'someone put a bug on your car when you were at the press conference. They must have guessed you might show up after all.'

Cold crept through Will's veins at her words, the enormity of the situation crashing through the last of the reassurances he'd created for himself over the past three days.

'We need to move, Will. Enough talking, okay?' Erin thrust his backpack at him, slid the phone parts off the bedside table and pushed them into his hand. 'Is that everything?'

'Bathroom. Razor.' Will mumbled, still trying to keep up with the turn of events.

He watched as she raced out of the room, and then returned with his razor and toothpaste.

'All the essentials, huh?' She managed a small smile as she handed them over.

'Something like that.' He dropped the items into the backpack, before following her to the door. 'Um – where are we going?'

'Somewhere safe.'

She turned and led the way out the room, down the corridor and towards the fire exit at the end, where she stopped, her hand on the door.

'Will? When we leave here, no asking questions, okay?'

He frowned, and waited for her to explain.

'We need to move fast. I've found another motel about two miles away. Paid cash,' she said. 'But we can't hang around. They'll know you're back from wherever you've been so they're going to be paying this place a visit soon. We have to hurry – I don't fancy our chances if they spot us leaving, do you?'

'Okay,' said Will, and set his shoulders. 'You're right.' He brushed past her, pushed the outer door open, and then looked down at her. 'Ladies first?'

She rolled her eyes, before ducking under his arm and out into the night.

Will followed, a hundred questions racing through his mind. 'I didn't know you had a car.'

'I don't. We're walking,' she said. 'How do you think I got this bloody wet in the first place?'

Chapter 26

Will pushed back into the shadows of the deserted petrol station, and cursed.

He was cold, wet, and out of breath after following Erin through a convoluted route of side streets and alleyways.

Halfway, she had stopped and thrust him against a tall wooden fence that bordered the gardens of a row of terraced houses.

A terrified cat had skittered away from them. Erin had watched it run, before turning her attention back to Will.

'Your backpack,' she'd hissed. 'Have you let it out of your sight since this all started?'

He'd shaken his head. 'No – why?'

She'd stepped back, and seemed to relax a little. 'The motel's only another half a mile away.' She pointed at his bag. 'No sense in leading them straight to us if they'd bugged your bag as well. I should've thought of it, back at the room.' She'd shrugged, a wave of misery clouding her features.

'Hey, it's okay,' Will had soothed. 'It's been with me all the time. Scout's honour.'

She'd nodded, and they'd started running again.

Now, the motel loomed in front of them, the bright lights of its reception area pooling over the car park. Only six vehicles filled the spaces, the spotlights from the building angled in such a way that would-be thieves would move on to easier targets.

'The room's round the back,' Erin murmured.

They both jumped as the sound of an approaching vehicle reached them.

Will pulled her back into the shadows with him, holding her close. She trembled under his touch, and he closed his eyes as the vehicle drew closer, tilting his face away from the approaching headlights.

The car passed them without stopping, its wheels splashing through the puddles on the asphalt. Spray soaked Will's jeans and he felt Erin relax in his arms.

He released her, and they smiled.

'Maybe we're getting a little too paranoid,' he suggested.

She shook her head. 'That's what's going to keep us alive,' she said. 'Come on.'

She slipped her hand into his, and they hurried across the road to the motel. She led him down the side of the building and through a smaller entranceway, then along a bright corridor painted in the motel chain's signature colours.

At a door halfway along, she stopped, pulled out a swipe card and pushed the door open.

Warmth radiated from the room, and Will sighed as he let the backpack slide from his shoulders.

Erin locked the door and padded into the living area, her wet shoes squeaking.

Will blushed. 'Look, I, um – without wanting to sound weird – we need to get out of these wet clothes.'

Erin nodded. 'You're right.' She walked over to a built-in wardrobe and slid the door open, then pulled out matching towels.

'Do you want to get in the shower first to warm up, or shall I?'

'You go first. I'll find something for us to lay out our clothes on to dry.'

'Okay.'

Will lowered his gaze as she made her way towards the bathroom, the purr of the extractor fan filling the awkward silence.

'Will?'

He raised his head. She stood in the doorway to the bathroom, a hesitant look on her face. He raised his eyebrow.

'Don't leave the room, okay?'

'Sure – we don't know if we're safe yet, right?'

'Yes. And I don't want to be left alone. I need to know that you're going to be here when I get out the shower. I need to know I'm going to be safe.'

'I'll be here.'

She nodded, then slipped into the bathroom and closed the door.

Will waited until he heard the shower taps squeak and water splashing against the tiles, then pulled his jacket off his shoulders and slung it over the back of a chair.

Bending down, he unzipped the backpack. He reached in and pulled out the hard drive and his mother's bible, then stood on tip-toe and slid them onto the top of one of the cabinets in the small kitchenette.

He stepped back to the bathroom door, and then turned, checking the angle. The hard drive and bible remained out of sight.

His heart pounded in his chest. If Erin looked for the items in his backpack when it was his turn to use the shower, would she question their whereabouts? Or did she trust him so much that she wouldn't seek them out in the first place? And why didn't he feel that he could trust her?

He sighed and ran a hand through his wet hair. The hiss of water from the bathroom stopped, the taps squeaked once, and the shower screen door slammed shut.

Will pulled his sweater and t-shirt over his head, the sodden material clammy under his fingers. He peeled off his socks, and then rummaged in the back of the wardrobe until he found a clothes rail, which he dragged across to the wall heater, before laying out his clothes.

He straightened as the bathroom door opened, and Erin appeared. He felt his breath catch in his throat.

She'd wrapped herself in one of the fluffy towels, her freshly washed hair tumbling into her eyes. She clutched her wet clothes against her chest.

He swallowed, her vulnerability cutting through him. 'Are you okay?' he managed.

She nodded. 'A bit better, yes.' A faint smile reached her lips. 'I think I even saved some hot water for you.'

Her gaze travelled over his naked chest, before she blinked, then stepped into the room. 'I'd better hang these up.'

'Sure.' Will moved away from the clothes drier, then reached across the bed and picked up the other towel. 'I guess I'd better warm up too.'

He hurried towards the bathroom, and shut the door. He exhaled, and tried to ignore the stirring below his waistband.

'Shower,' he mumbled. 'Maybe cold.'

He stripped off his jeans and boxer shorts, kicking them to the floor, then wiped the palm of his hand over the fogged glass of the mirror.

A gaunt, tired man looked back at him through haunted eyes. Dark circles had appeared under his lids, and he tried to remember when he'd last had a decent night's sleep.

He scowled at his expression, turned, and stepped into the shower, turning the taps on full.

He let out an involuntary groan as the hot water hit his skin, before he made liberal use of the soap and shampoo.

When he stepped out five minutes later, he was pink, and the room was filled with a light mist.

The extractor fan continued to purr in its pathetic attempts to clear the fog, and Will pulled the thick material of the towel around his waist. Picking up his clothes, he opened the door and switched off the fan.

The main room was darker. Erin had switched off the harsh overhead lights and instead, both bedside lights were glowing.

The clothes drier had bent slightly under the weight of the wet clothes, so Will put his jeans on the back of a second chair and tucked his pants next to them.

Erin sat on the small sofa, watching. ‘I figured you wouldn’t fit on here, so you can have the bed, if you want.’

Will glanced at the double bed, its inviting cotton sheets and blankets and the quilt that covered the lower half. He cleared his throat, and cursed inwardly at the heat he knew rose in his cheeks.

‘Look, we’re both tired,’ he began. ‘We both need to rest. Why don’t we just share the bed?’

She stood then, and crossed the room to him.

‘Okay.’

Chapter 27

Ian Rossiter stared at the amber liquid at the bottom of the crystal glass, eyed the bottle of twenty-year-old malt on the corner of his desk, and then changed his mind.

He pushed the glass away, rested his elbows on the desk and pinched the bridge of his nose. He glared at the oak panelled door that led into his office, and waited.

Ten hours ago, Gregory had slipped into the room, closed the door and confirmed his two hired thugs had located Will Fletcher.

They had followed him to the church in Bracklewood but he'd escaped. They had let him run, rightly assuming that they could simply follow the GPS tracker fixed to the underside of his car.

The fact that Fletcher had suddenly become mobile and left the city originally confused Gregory's intelligence sources, until they had clarified that he'd borrowed the car from a work colleague at the museum before turning up to the press conference.

Rossiter grunted. He had to give Gregory credit. If he hadn't arranged for the tracking device to be fitted to the car, they'd have had no way of finding the man. Not without raising suspicion.

Then, eight hours ago, the two men had contacted them once more.

Fletcher had arrived at a motel, and they had parked in a side street opposite the car park. They'd watched as he'd locked the car and entered the building via a side door.

'What about his backpack?' Rossiter had asked.

Gregory had held up his hand and relayed the question to his contact, before shaking his head. 'No good,' he'd said. 'He took it inside with him.'

They'd agreed the men should wait and watch the motel from their vantage point.

Gregory had discovered the reception duty manager's shift changed at four o'clock in the morning and it was decided the two thugs would enter the building fifteen minutes before, while the receptionist was more likely to be distracted by the thought of handing over to the morning shift and getting some sleep.

Rossiter rubbed at his eyes and glanced at his watch. Only minutes to go now.

Gregory had urged him to get some rest, his argument being that if Rossiter had to face the news cameras again, he'd better look presentable.

Rossiter had dismissed the suggestion vehemently.

'No – let them see me looking like shit,' he'd growled. 'It'll make my injury look more realistic.'

Gregory had shrugged. 'It's your choice,' he'd said. 'But I'm going back to my office to get my head down. I'll wake you when we've got some news.'

'Make sure you do.'

Rossiter had waited until the door had clicked shut, then launched himself at the liquor cabinet.

The first measure had simply served to wash the painkillers down his throat.

He'd taken his time with the second, larger, measure, adding ice and watching the cubes melt into the alcohol as the night progressed.

He shifted in his chair and groaned as the stitches in his shoulder protested, and vowed to take it easier, once the election was over.

He heard Gregory's voice outside in the hallway a brief moment before the man burst into the room, his phone pressed to his ear, his face pale.

Rossiter's heart lurched in his chest as he saw the man's expression, adrenalin surging through his veins.

Gregory stumbled across the carpeted floor, then turned and slammed the door shut, before he hastened towards Rossiter, still talking.

'No, no – I understand. What's that?' His eyes widened. 'No! Absolutely not. I repeat, do not pursue that course of action. Not unless I sanction it.'

Rossiter rose, standing behind his desk, his palms planted on the surface, sweat pooling onto the mahogany under his fingers.

He longed to take the phone from Gregory, to find out what was happening. The terror in the man's eyes spoke volumes.

Either the mission hadn't gone ahead as planned, or something had gone very wrong.

He forced air into his lungs, stared at the man in front of him, and waited.

Gregory ran his hand through his hair, appeared to freeze for a moment, and then sprang into action once more.

'Okay. I'll tell you what to do. Drive around, check out the other motels in the area. He can't have gone far without his car. Keep me posted.'

Rossiter closed his eyes as Gregory ended the call.

He sank back into his chair and pinched the bridge of his nose. He heard Gregory slump into one of the armchairs on the other side of the desk, and opened his eyes.

'What went wrong?'

Gregory didn't waste time with detail. The less Rossiter knew about how his people broke into buildings in search of people or property, the more deniable his involvement remained.

'He wasn't there.'

'Then where is he?'

'They don't know.'

'Explain.'

Gregory sighed. 'When they got to the room, it was empty. It looks like he left in a hurry. The bed hasn't been slept in today, but the bathroom had been used.'

'How long has he been missing for?'

'They're not sure. They didn't see him leave.'

'Shit.' Rossiter pushed back his chair and began to pace the room.

'There's something else.'

'What?'

Gregory held up his phone. 'Will Fletcher had a visitor last night, before he disappeared.'

Rossiter snatched the phone from the man's grasp and stared at the photograph.

'It seems Mr Fletcher may have had some help from your niece,' said Gregory.

Rossiter ignored the note of smugness in the man's voice.

Blood rushed in his ears and he blinked away the tiredness that only moments before had threatened sleep. Fury consumed him as he held the phone closer and glared at the image.

It was definitely Erin, her long hair wet from the rain that fell in swathes onto the concrete perimeter of the motel.

The photographer had captured her as she was raising her hand to push open the door of the side entrance to the building, her head turned towards him as she'd checked over her shoulder to see if she was being followed.

'Do they know who she is?' he asked, his eyes flicking to Gregory before returning to the image.

'No. I haven't told them, and they've never met her.'

Rossiter threw the phone onto the desk with such force that the screen shattered.

'I'll kill her,' he snarled.

Chapter 28

Will woke up with a start, the sun's rays bleaching the curtains, pooling through the gap between them and over the tumbled sheets.

He lifted his head, rubbed his eyes, and then swore under his breath at the limbs entangled around him.

His towel lay twisted under his body.

Memories of the previous night flooded back, tinged with an overwhelming guiltiness while he tried to remember if anything had transpired.

He glanced down. Erin's head rested on his bare torso, her breath tickling the hairs on his chest, while the sheet had peeled back to expose her collar bone, the porcelain skin almost translucent in the morning light.

He let his head drop back onto the pillow and closed his eyes.

Now what?

'Well, this is awkward,' mumbled a voice against his shoulder, before Erin shuffled away from him, the towel discarded, and a grin plastered across her face.

'Um, yeah – it is a bit.' Will ignored the sensation that swept over him at the sight of her naked body, and hugged the sheets tighter to his chest. 'Sorry.'

She shrugged. 'Don't apologise.' She swung her legs over the side of the bed and tossed her hair over her shoulder on the way to the bathroom. 'It was rather nice.'

As the sound of water gushing over the tiles reached the bed, Will groaned then got up and pulled on his clothes, rubbing his hand over the rough stubble that covered his jaw. Showering would have to wait.

He checked over his shoulder that Erin was still in the shower, and then slipped Amy's mobile phone from where he'd tucked it under the mattress upon arriving at the room the night before.

He hit the playback button for the voicemail, and listened to Amy's voice fill the void again, the guilt even stronger. After listening twice, he turned off the phone and dropped it into his jacket pocket, then leaned over and plucked the handset up off the room landline.

While he waited to be connected to Amy's specialist, he started to make a mental list of what he and Erin would need to do that morning – starting with coffee. Somewhere in there was a conversation about setting some new ground rules too, if they were going to be anywhere near each other for the foreseeable future.

'Hathaway.'

'Mr Hathaway, good morning – it's Will Fletcher. I wondered how Amy was doing.'

Will heard the surgeon sit back in his leather chair, and imagined the man putting his feet up on the desk, harried, overworked and exhausted. The tiredness echoed down the line when he eventually spoke.

'Will, good morning,' he paused, and Will held his breath before the man continued. 'Amy didn't have such a good night,' he said. 'We've stabilised her for now, but the swelling on her brain hasn't reduced, and we've got her under continuous observation.'

'I'm out of town at the moment,' said Will. 'Sorting out some family stuff. Should I come back straight away?'

'I'll phone you if the situation changes,' said Hathaway. 'I'll be honest, though, Will, the next twenty-four hours are going to be critical.'

'They are, that's true,' Will replied, and disconnected the call. 'So, what do we do now?'

Erin stood with her hands on her hips, staring out the window. She turned at his words.

'Only you can answer that, Will,' she said. 'I've got us somewhere safe to stay. You need to find out why we're hiding – and fast.' She pointed at the computer, then picked up her bag. 'It's going to take you a while to go through that,' she said. 'I'm going to wander down to the café – see if I can find us something to eat.'

'Okay,' he said absently, lost in thought as she closed the door on her way out.

Will waited until she'd closed the door behind her before he hurried across to the cabinet where he'd hidden the hard drive and bible the night before.

He put the hard drive in his backpack, then sat on the edge of the bed and ran his thumb over the worn cover of the decades-old book.

He rubbed his finger over a faded inscription on the first page, a fleeting recollection of his grandmother's writing on his birthday cards, before he began to flick through the pages.

The obvious place to start looking was to search for any passages in the bible that had been marked or highlighted.

Will sighed. He wasn't sure what he was looking for, except that he'd seen it done in films so it seemed a good place to begin.

After five minutes, Erin reappeared, padded over the carpet, placed two Styrofoam coffee cups on the desk, and sat next to him.

'What's that?'

'My mum's bible.'

'Oh.'

Will swallowed, knowing his next decision could very well end his life if his instincts were wrong about the woman beside him.

'Amy hid it – at the church where Colin Avery is buried.'

'Who's he?'

Will moved to the little desk, and then handed the print-out of the three photographs to her. 'Someone that Rossiter and Gregory were involved with. I think in Northern Ireland first. He was a mercenary.'

Erin's eyebrows shot up. 'What happened to him?'

'The vicar at the church told me Avery died when a bomb he was building blew up in his face.' Will shrugged. 'Needless to say, he wasn't very sympathetic.'

Erin tapped the earlier photograph with her fingernail. 'What on earth would they be doing hanging around with a mercenary?'

Will shrugged. 'I don't know – security maybe? I mean, they seem to have easy access to the sort of people that can track vehicles, don't they?'

Erin pursed her lips. 'And maybe they used those same people to carry out the attack on Monday.'

'It sounds like a possibility.'

Erin handed back the photographs. 'Why would Amy hide the bible at the church where Colin Avery is buried, though? What's so dangerous that she couldn't just tell you to get it from your mum?'

'I think she left me a clue in here somewhere. And I think she was scared these people might do something to my mum to get it. She told my mother that she'd left it somewhere safe, so it must be important to her investigation.'

He continued to flick through the pages, the thin paper creasing under his touch.

He ran his fingers over the inside back cover of the book, lost in thought, and then glanced down.

The material had puckered around the edges, as if it had been damp at some point. Towards the spine, a jagged edge stuck out from the otherwise neat saddle-stitched pages.

He glanced sideways at Erin, who was staring at the seam.

'Go on,' she urged.

He ran his finger over the cut, before he tried to lift the binding. His finger broke the seal, and he realised the inner cover had been sliced open, and then glued back together.

His heart racing, he gently peeled back the rest of the paper until he could slip his fingers inside. They grasped a separate piece of paper – thicker in consistency, and he carefully extracted it.

He put the bible on the bed next to him and unfolded the lined notepaper, his breathing shallow with expectation.

'What the…?'

In his hands, Amy's writing looped across the page, except he was holding it upside down. He turned it between his fingers.

A name, and an address were printed neatly across the lines, together with a message from Amy.

Find this man, Will. He has what you need.

Chapter 29

Will stood at the bus stop and lifted his gaze from the newspaper he held.

Across the road, another hundred yards away, a group of smokers sat huddled around a collection of tables under an awning outside a pub, their cigarette smoke wafting on the wind that rattled down the street.

He'd reached the address Amy had left for him, only to see the occupant slam the front door shut and begin walking away in the opposite direction.

For a moment, Will considered waiting until the man returned, except that the terraced houses had no front gardens, he'd had to park the rental car half a mile away, and there was nowhere else to wait without the neighbours becoming suspicious.

By the time he'd made up his mind to follow the man, his quarry was at the end of the road and about to turn the corner.

He'd jogged to catch up, and then followed him along a busy road lined with a mixture of larger houses and an occasional shop. The man turned left once more, and then Will groaned as the man had stopped and pushed open the door of a pub.

Realising he could be in for a long wait, he'd spied the bus shelter farther down the road on the opposite side and had picked up a discarded newspaper from the bench seat.

The man had emerged with a pint glass in his hand – Will guessed it to be his second – after forty minutes, and proceeded to join the small group of smokers outside, his back to the bus stop.

When he'd suggested to Erin that she accompany him, she'd shaken her head.

'No – this is something you have to do,' she'd said. 'Besides, both of us turning up to question him might frighten him off, don't you think?'

In the end, he'd agreed, but had made her lock the door as he'd left, with the promise she wouldn't open it to anyone in his absence.

After half an hour and two buses, he wondered whether he should move. He couldn't stay any longer without becoming suspicious.

On the other hand, he tried to reason with himself, maybe the man only had two pints of beer at mid-day.

He jerked his head sideways at the rumble of an approaching bus.

It wheezed to a standstill, and an elderly couple clambered down its steps onto the pavement, calling their thanks to the driver as they wandered away.

'Do you want this one?' asked the driver.

Will shook his head, and the doors hissed closed.

As the bus drew away, his attention went back to the pub across the street.

He blinked.

The man was no longer sitting at the smokers' table.

Will dropped the newspaper to the seat and leaned forward.

Had he gone back inside for another drink?

As the bus reached the end of the street and turned right, Will's eyes caught the flap of an overcoat as the man turned the corner.

'Shit!'

Will sprinted along the pavement, and then checked over his shoulder to make sure the road was clear and dashed across both lanes. He slowed as he reached the corner, and edged round it.

The man was strolling back along the busy street, in the direction of his home.

Will wanted to make sure he caught up with the man on his front door step. He didn't want to cause a scene on the street in front of all the neighbours, not until he worked out if the man could help him – and what his relationship to Amy's story was.

As they turned right and entered the street of terraced houses once more, Will quickened his pace so that by the time the man reached into his pocket and drew out his keys, he was within speaking distance without having to raise his voice.

'Mackenzie Harris?'

The man's head shot round, a hunted expression on his face.

He turned the key in the lock, and pushed the door open.

Will didn't want to miss his chance. He stepped forward, his arm out to stop the door from being shut, and was taken aback when the man turned, grabbed his arm and dragged him into the house, slamming the door behind them.

The strength of the older man took him by surprise. The man shoved Will hard against the wall of the hallway, his arm across his throat.

Will's head hit a picture frame with the force of the man's weight against him, and he flinched as the hard wooden surface struck the base of his skull.

'Who the fuck are you?'

Will held his hands up in front of him. 'Will Fletcher,' he gasped. 'Amy Peters told me you'd help me.'

Recognition flickered in the man's eyes, and he lowered his arm. 'Say that again.'

'Amy – she said you'd help me.'

The man stepped back. 'Did she now? Did she speak to you?'

Will shook his head, kept one had raised, and reached into his pocket. 'She left this for me. It was hidden.'

He held out the piece of paper with Amy's handwriting on it.

The old man's hand shook as he took it, reading the message twice before giving it back. 'I think we need to have a talk, Will Fletcher.' He held out his hand. 'I'm Mackenzie Harris. You can call me Mack,' he said. 'Sorry about the dramatics, but I have to be very careful about who calls me that these days.'

'I don't understand,' said Will. 'Isn't that your name?'

Mack shrugged off his overcoat and hung it on a hook on the wall next to the door. 'I haven't been called that for a long time, Will.' He gestured towards the back of the house. 'Come on, I'll put the kettle on.'

Will followed him along the gloomy passageway, the wallpaper peeling off the walls at the corners. He raised his eyes to the ceiling and saw damp patches yellowing the once-white paintwork, the dank smell filling his senses as they passed underneath.

The threadbare carpet gave way to linoleum as they entered the kitchen, the plastic surface sticky under the soles of Will's shoes.

The older man made tea, handed Will a chipped mug full of the strong brew, and gestured towards the front living room.

Will sank into one of the thinly-stuffed arm chairs while Mack patted the pockets of his cardigan before extracting a crumpled packet of cigarettes.

He tapped one into the palm of his hand, then scrunched up the packet and stuffed it back into his pocket before easing into his armchair. Reaching out for a cigarette lighter on a small table next to his chair, he finally spoke.

'So Amy's in hospital, then?'

Will nodded and looked at his hands. 'It didn't sound very good when I last spoke with her surgeon,' he said.

Mack tipped his head back and exhaled a plume of smoke towards the ceiling. 'That's a damn shame to hear, lad. A damn shame.'

'I was hoping you could help me. I need to find out what she found out.' Will broke off, his voice choked. 'I need to make this stop.'

'They're after you now, I presume?'

'Yeah.' His eyes met Mack's. 'How much do you know about what's been going on?'

The man held his stare. 'Everything, lad.' He took another drag on his cigarette. 'Everything.'

As he turned to tap his cigarette on the edge of the ashtray, Will slumped in the chair, finally recognising him.

'You're the fourth man in the photograph I have, aren't you?'

Chapter 30

Mack nodded.

'Why?'

'I worked with them.'

Will leaned forward, his heart racing. 'Recently?'

Mack shook his head. 'A long time ago. Before Rossiter got it into his head that he could be Prime Minister.' He sighed, a trace of smoke chasing his words. 'Now *that's* a fucked up idea, if I've ever heard one.'

'What did you do for them?'

Mack looked away, his gaze falling on the logs burning in the fireplace. He stubbed out the cigarette in an ashtray beside him and rubbed his hand over his chin. 'I was an enforcer.'

Will's eyes narrowed. 'You mean you tortured people?'

'No,' said Mack and lowered his gaze to his hands. 'I didn't have the stomach for that. I just roughed people up a bit – the ones that owed money or needed a bit of convincing to sign deals.'

'How did you get involved?'

'I needed the money.' The older man shrugged. 'I'd been a boxer in my youth. Pretty good. Took a fall too many, and my career was over by the time I was twenty-two.'

'So you became a criminal?'

'Lad, when everyone else in your neighbourhood is taking turns to blow things to shit, you do what you have to,' Mack snapped. 'It's not like I had a lot of choice.'

Will frowned. 'I don't remember anything in Amy's notes about Rossiter being paramilitary,' he said. 'I thought he worked in construction.'

Mack fidgeted in his seat, pulled out the cigarette packet, and lit up. 'I'm not talking about paramilitary groups, Will,' he said, putting the packet next to the ashtray. 'I'm talking about organised crime.'

'What, like the mafia?'

Mack cackled, and then started to cough. 'Oh, if we were that organised, we would have done some real damage.' He shook his head. 'No – once the Royal Ulster Constabulary got disbanded, there were a few months where the politicians had their heads up their arses, all trying to agree how a new Northern Ireland police service would work. Everyone had to have their say-so, of course.' He took a drag on the cigarette, his yellow fingers shaking. 'In the meantime, a few enterprising men took advantage.' He shrugged. 'You can check out the statistics yourself with your…' he mimed typing with his fingers, 'internet search or whatever. Crime shot up after 1998. Made some people rich men. Very rich men.'

He leaned forward and glared at Will. 'And some of those very rich men are now very *powerful* men. And they don't want people like your girlfriend digging up their past.'

'Hang on, Ian Rossiter isn't Irish – nor is Gregory. So why the hell do I have a copy of a photograph showing you with them and Colin Avery in camouflage?'

'Rossiter could see the writing was on the wall for the smaller groups running around with guns,' said Mack. 'The ones who were never going to get a say-so in the whole devolution process. He started out by offering work to some of them. Y'know – security at construction sites, debt collecting rents, that sort of thing.'

'What was he doing over in Belfast, though? Isn't he from Liverpool?'

'He saw an opportunity,' explained Mack. 'Or so he told me. Thing is, once they stopped blowing buildings up and started talking to each other instead, there was a lot of money to be made in redevelopment and construction across Northern Ireland. He got in early, made his mark, and got out quick before the authorities caught up with him.'

'Where does Gregory come into all this?'

Mack cursed under his breath, and Will was taken aback at the profanity that escaped the older man's lips.

'He's the real brains of the whole set-up,' said Mack once he'd got his temper back under control. 'And just as dangerous. He ran the money side of the business for Rossiter – and his security. As far as I can tell, he still does.'

'I wonder who's idea it was for Rossiter to run for Prime Minister?'

'Gregory I expect. He always was the more ambitious of the two, but Rossiter's more photogenic.' Mack shrugged. 'Gregory would be more than comfortable acting as deputy. He'll be pulling strings in the background, though, mark my words.'

Will leaned back in his chair and ran his hands through his hair. 'I still can't understand why they'd kill to cover that up, though – I mean, okay, it might cost him the election, but arranging to *murder* someone? There must've been something else going on.'

'Like what? Got any ideas?

'No. There's nothing else in Amy's notes. I don't understand why she thought I'd work out what she had found.'

Mack's eyes narrowed. 'Well, you seem to have been doing all right so far. Who's helping you?'

Will wondered whether he should tell the old man about Erin's involvement, and then figured he'd probably find out somehow anyway.

'Rossiter's niece.'

It was Mack's turn to be surprised. 'Really? What's her name?'

'Erin.'

'Do you trust her?'

'Yes, I do. She's already saved me once from Rossiter's hired thugs.'

The older man grunted and pointed at the fireplace. 'Put another log on that, would you? I'm too comfortable to move.'

Will rose from the chair and walked the short distance to the hearth. He leaned down, picked out a log, and slung it onto the fire, before straightening. As he was about to turn back to the room, one of the photographs on the mantelpiece caught his attention, and all thought of what he was going to ask Mack froze in his throat.

The silence filled the room, until Mack's voice reached him.

'So, you see, I've known Erin for quite a while.'

Will stared at the framed photograph in his hand of a man and a small girl, no more than five years old. She clutched a teddy bear, thumb in mouth, while the man pointed at the camera, trying to get her to smile for the photographer.

'She's your *daughter*?' he said, holding up the frame. 'When the hell were you going to tell me?'

'Like you said yourself,' said Mack. 'We didn't know if we could trust you.'

'So, what's this all about? A family vendetta or something?'

Mack nodded slowly, his gaze never leaving Will's. 'That's *exactly* what this is.' He stabbed his finger at Will. 'And Amy decided to use it to her advantage.'

Will sank back into the armchair, setting the photograph on the small coffee table next to it. He stared at it for a moment longer, and then tore his gaze away to face Mack.

'What do you mean, Amy *used* it?'

Mack slumped back into his own chair and rubbed his hand across his eyes. When he lowered his arm, Will noticed tears glistening in the corners of the man's eyes and waited.

The older man took a shuddering breath before speaking again.

'Ian Rossiter molested my little girl,' he whispered. 'I didn't know. I *swear* I didn't know until she told me.' A gasp escaped his lips, and he reached into his trouser pocket and extracted a paper tissue, dabbed at his eyes, and then blew his nose.

'Jesus, Mack – I'm so sorry,' murmured Will and looked at his hands.

He waited until the older man's sobs quietened, then raised his head. 'Is this why you agreed to help Amy?'

Mack nodded. 'No one would ever believe Erin if she tried to tell them what he did – he's got too many powerful friends who would rush to his aid and rubbish her story.' He blew his nose again, then stood and threw the paper tissue into the hearth.

Will stared into the flames as the tissue flared and caught fire, the material quickly turning to ash.

'Why didn't you report him?' he asked. 'Why didn't you do something?'

Mack sniffled, picked up the brass poker and jabbed at the logs in the grate. 'Because I was too damn scared,' he said. 'I don't know how Amy found me,' he added. 'When I moved over here, I changed my name and laid low for a few years. Managed to get Erin into a small village school without someone asking too many questions.'

He straightened, and Will saw the fear in the man's eyes. 'Ian Rossiter isn't someone you just go to the police and expect help,' Mack said. 'He was terrifying back then – now he's got too many friends in high places these days.'

Mack leaned down and put the poker back into the bucket next to the fireplace, before returning to his armchair with a sigh.

'I don't think your girlfriend knew about Rossiter's preference for young girls when she met Erin,' he said 'I think she had something else on him – some sort of story she was chasing anyway. Then once they started talking, Erin opened up and told her about the abuse. It was Amy who persuaded her to tell me.'

He used the sleeve of his cardigan to wipe his eyes once more.

The shrill ring of the phone in Will's backpack made them both jump.

'Shit,' said Will. 'I thought I'd switched that off.' He mumbled an apology, leaned over, and pulled out Amy's mobile. His own work number was displayed on the screen.

After three rings, the phone fell silent.

'Do you need to phone someone back?' asked Mack, squinting through the cigarette smoke that swirled around his face.

Will nodded. 'I have to step outside,' he said and hurried from the room, slipping the backpack over his shoulder as he went.

Closing the front door, he walked to the end of the street, hunkering into his thin jacket against the wind.

He glanced over his shoulder and drew out the mobile phone. His heart beating, he glanced at the phone number, wondering what his boss, Jack, would want at such an hour.

'It's Will – were you after me?' he said when the older man picked up the call.

'Will, thank god. We've been trying to reach you since yesterday. I tried Amy's phone on the off-chance you might have it.'

'Sorry, the battery in mine had gone flat,' Will lied. 'What's wrong?'

Jack breathed out shakily, and Will heard the familiar squeak of the man's leather office chair as he sat. 'Russell Harper's been killed in an accident.'

Will pulled the phone away from his ear and fought the bile down in his throat. His eyes stung, and he took deep breaths to ward off the dizziness that was threatening to engulf him.

'When? I mean, how?'

'Yesterday afternoon. He'd left the office on an errand or something. It's a bit odd. He told the security guard downstairs to call the police if he didn't return within the hour.'

Jack sniffled and put the phone down, and Will heard him blow his nose before returning to the phone. 'Sorry, it's all a bit of a shock. Anyway, it looks like he was on his way back to the museum from wherever he'd been and was waiting to cross the junction at Russell Square when a bus went past,' he said. 'One of the witnesses said a man in the crowd at the pavement waiting to cross might have pushed him, but no one else saw it so the police can't prove anything.'

Will's legs began to shake, and he looked around for something to lean against, settling on a low wall covered in graffiti.

Russell had been right, then. He was already being followed. And killed because he emailed a photograph to a friend.

Will gulped in fresh air, the ramifications of what had happened hitting him. It meant Rossiter's cronies were monitoring his emails as well. He cleared his throat.

'Don't they have CCTV cameras everywhere?'

'Apparently the bus was blocking its view,' said Jack. 'We're all in shock here. I've got no idea why he told the security guard to call the police if he didn't turn up either – have you?'

Will shook his head, then realised he had to speak. 'No,' he murmured.

Jack sighed. 'They asked if he was a drug user. I think they were suggesting it was a drug deal gone wrong. That he was killed by his supplier.'

'Russell didn't use drugs,' Will assured him. 'He was very much anti-drugs – I think a mate of his overdosed when he was a teenager.'

'That's what I thought.' Jack said, his voice relieved. 'The police say the coroner's hearing has been set for next month, but it sounds like it's going to be recorded as an accidental death unless someone comes forward with information.'

'Jesus.' Will leaned forward and held his head in his hands, the phone pressed tight to his ear.

'Where are you anyway?' asked Jack. 'Have you been to see Amy?'

Will coughed. 'Ah, no, not yet.' He stood and began to pace the pavement. 'She's still in intensive care, so the surgeon's keeping me posted.'

'How is she?'

'Not good. I'm going to phone them for an update in a moment.'

'Okay.' Jack sighed. 'I'll get off the phone so you can do that. I'll give you a call when I've got the details for Russell's funeral.'

'Thanks, Jack. I'll talk to you soon.'

Will ended the call, then turned away from the wall and began to walk.

The wind picked up, buffeting him as he stalked along the pavement, lost in thought. A gust tugged his hair across his face and he pushed it out of his eyes, scowling as he tried to digest the news.

Reaching a bus shelter, he slumped onto the aluminium seat and dialled the number for the hospital, then waited to be put through to the nurse's station outside the intensive care unit.

He introduced himself to the nurse who answered, then waited while she fetched Amy's notes.

He jumped when Hathaway's voice came on the line.

'Will? Are you in town?'

'No – I, um, had to catch up with family – I'm a few hours away at the moment. What's wrong?'

The surgeon sighed. 'Look, Will, I'll be honest. It's not good. Amy's developed an infection. We're going to keep her in intensive care until we can be absolutely sure she's out of danger, but that could be days, maybe weeks.'

'Is – is there anything I should do?' Will bit his lip, trying to stop the tremble in his voice. 'I mean, I can get there this evening if you think…' He cleared his throat. 'If you think I need to be there, you know, in case…'

'It would be better, although I do understand if you have other family issues to resolve,' said the surgeon. 'But, please – do try to phone every few hours if you can.'

'I will.'

'Good, well, talk to you soon.'

The surgeon hung up, and Will stared at the phone in his hand for a moment before pulling it apart and putting the pieces in his pocket once more.

He rested his elbows on his knees and stared into the road, his thoughts racing, before he stood, brushed off the back of his jeans, and strode back in the direction of the Irishman's house.

If he was going to avenge Simon and Russell's deaths and make some sense of why Amy still lay in an induced coma, he had some work to do.

Chapter 31

'How much of this do you think Amy found out?'

Mack shrugged. 'Must have been close. I reckon Rossiter panicked.'

He poured generous measures into two glasses, screwed the cap back on the whiskey bottle, and shuffled across the room to Will, who took one of the drinks from him.

'It seems a bit extreme: killing four people now, putting a fifth in an induced coma, and getting himself shot in the process.' He took a sip of the amber liquid, the smooth burn in his throat doing little to calm his nerves, despite Mack's assurances it would help.

'Do you doubt me?'

'No – no, I believe you. I just think he must've had help from someone else. Hell of a job to attack a politician's car in broad daylight and shoot him.'

Mack shrugged. 'Used to do it all the time.'

Will cocked an eyebrow. 'Do I want to hear about it?'

'Probably not.' Mack sighed and rubbed a hand over his face. 'Look, it's late. I'm tired. Can we talk about this some more in the morning?'

Will stood, shouldering his backpack. 'Sure, whatever.' He pulled his car keys from his pocket.

'Put those away. You can have the spare room. There's not a hotel to be found for at least ten miles from here.'

Will bit his lip. 'Are you sure?'

Mack laughed. 'Don't worry, lad. I'm not going to murder you in your sleep.'

Will exhaled, unwilling to admit that was *exactly* what had been going through his head. 'Okay.'

He followed Mack out of the living area and up a narrow flight of stairs, each one creaking, the carpet threadbare.

'You should get these stair treads fixed,' said Will as they ascended. 'They sound awful.'

Mack stopped halfway up and glared at Will. 'They sound awful, as you put it, because they act as an early warning system.' He turned and stamped up the remaining stairs. 'If someone decides to try and murder me in *my* sleep, I'd hear them coming.'

Will swallowed, realised his hands were shaking, and grasped hold of the bannister before jogging up the stairs to join Mack on the small landing.

'Right,' said Mack, ignoring his discomfort. 'Bathroom's there – I'm in that room, and this is yours.'

He swung open the door to a room filled with boxes, their contents spilled out onto the floor. A worn sofa took up one length of wall under a window. Mack tugged the curtains closed and pointed at the sofa.

'That's a bed. You sort it out – I'm too old to bend down there. I'll go and find some blankets.'

Will stared as he stomped from the room, then exhaled and crouched down until he could work out how the sofa-bed opened out. By the time he'd flattened it, then sat and tested the mattress, groaning at the thought of how his back would be playing up in the morning, Mack had returned.

He thrust a pillow and two blankets at Will. 'That should do you. I'm an early riser, so I'll see you when you wake up.'

He turned and left the room.

'Mack?'

'What?' The man appeared at the door, frowning.

'Thanks.'

'Whatever.'

Will stood, made the bed, and then stripped down to his boxers. Somehow, he didn't think sleep would come easily that night.

***

Will blinked, rubbed his hands over his eyes, and panicked, trying to work out where he was, until he remembered.

He sat up in the bed, blinked at the light creeping through the curtains, and decided that the blackbird chirping outside the window was too damn cheerful for such a cold morning.

Pulling on his clothes, he tossed back the blankets to air the sofa bed, and then sniffed.

Someone was cooking, and it smelled good.

He padded down the stairs, following the scent of bacon and eggs, until he found Mack in the kitchen, spatula in hand, shovelling fried tomatoes and mushrooms onto plates.

'Ah, he's alive and well,' he said, then nodded towards the kitchen bench. 'Help yourself to coffee. Milk's in the fridge.'

Will waited until the first caffeine rush hit his senses. 'Is there anything I can do?'

'No. Stay out of the way.'

Mack took the frying pan off the heat and dashed over to the toaster where a thin trail of smoke was escaping. 'Bollocks.'

He punched a button on the front of the toaster, before flapping a tea-towel at a smoke detector next to the door.

'Okay,' he said, dropping a plate in front of Will. 'Dig in.'

Will's stomach rumbled, and it was some time before the two men spoke again.

'How well did you get to know Amy?' Will asked as he put his utensils on the empty plate and pushed it to one side. He wrapped his fingers round his still-warm coffee mug and watched as Mack swept a slice of bread around the remaining juices on his own plate.

The older man shrugged, stuffed the bread in his mouth, and washed it down with a swig of coffee before speaking.

'She's a good journalist,' he said. 'She doesn't give up.' He sighed contentedly, pointed at the dishes, and then stood. 'Put those in the sink. I'll wash up later. Come on through to the front room where it's warmer.'

Will followed him through the house and collapsed into the same armchair he'd taken the previous night.

Mack stirred up the small fire he'd lit that morning and threw another log onto it before settling into his chair.

'Amy contacted me about six months ago,' he began. 'I've got no idea how she found me, but she did.' He shrugged. 'After I crossed the Sea twenty years ago, I settled here.'

'Why did you leave?'

Mack shrugged. 'Things were changing. I guess I was never into all that political shit. I saw an opportunity to make a fast profit while they were all sorting themselves out in the late nineties, but that only lasted a couple of years. By 2001, they were starting to cotton onto a lot of the criminal gangs. It was only a matter of time before I got caught.'

'Did you?'

'No. I was lucky,' said Mack. 'And smart. I never got greedy. And I made sure I got myself some insurance.'

'The sort of insurance people would kill for?'

'Yes.' Mack looked away and stared into the flames, before he turned back. 'So, Will Fletcher,' he said, tapping his fingers on the armrest. 'You came to me for help. I've told you everything I know. I think it's about time you tell me what you've been up to.'

The floodgates opened then, and Will found he couldn't stop talking. He told Mack about the mysterious phone calls, Simon's murder, Russell being run over by a bus, and the fact that he believed he was being followed.

Will ran his hand through his hair and sighed. 'What I don't understand is why you want to go after Rossiter now, after all these years? You could've said something about this ages ago.'

Mack shrugged. 'I didn't feel a need to, until now.'

'Because Rossiter's suddenly running for Parliament you mean?'

'No.' Mack coughed, leaned forward, and stubbed out the cigarette in the ashtray. 'Because I'm dying.'

'Great. This is your way of trying to absolve yourself, is it?'

The older man launched from his armchair at a speed belying his age.

Will's head snapped back as the force of Mack's open hand met his cheek. Tears welled up in his eyes, and he gasped as he clutched his face, the skin red, raw, and hot.

'Fuck you.' Mack stalked back to his armchair, wheezing.

Will sniffled a couple of times, and then raised his head. A wave of mild dizziness blurred his vision, and he blinked. He exhaled, a deep calming breath while his mind processed what he was hearing. He leaned back in his chair and tucked his hands behind his head, contemplating the ceiling.

Then it hit him.

He leaned forward and narrowed his eyes at Mack. 'You gave your 'insurance' to Amy, didn't you?'

'No.'

It came out as a whisper, and Will understood. Mack blamed himself for what had happened to Amy.

'What, then?'

Mack remained still, the silence stretching out between them, until he finally spoke. 'I told her about it, that's all. It was enough.'

Will ran over the facts in his mind – everything the man had told him so far. Then it clicked.

'You've got something else on Rossiter and Gregory, haven't you?'

'Yes.'

'What is it?

'Another photograph.'

Will's jaw dropped. 'Another photograph?' He leaned forward. '*What* photograph?'

Mack stubbed out his cigarette, blew the last of the smoke up towards the ceiling, and turned to Will, his eyes gleaming.

'The one your father took of Ian Rossiter executing one of his business rivals.'

Chapter 32

Belfast, Northern Ireland – Autumn 1999

The first thought that struck the nine-year-old boy as he ignored his mother's shout from the kitchen was that he should have listened to his parent's advice and not opened the door to strangers.

The second was that the man standing in front of him was holding a gun.

A really big gun.

Behind the man, rain hissed onto the garden path, the faint mist that filled the air blurring the white street light beyond the garden gate.

The boy dropped his robot toy to the floor, its complicated way of turning from car to robot and back forgotten as the tall stranger glared at him from eye-slits cut into a black woollen mask which covered his face.

A split second passed as realisation set in, then the man pushed him backwards, knocking him to the floor, and ran towards the kitchen where the boy's father stood, a towel hanging between his fingers where he'd been washing his hands before supper, his mouth open in shock.

The boy crawled out of the way, pushing his back against the freshly painted wall of the narrow hallway as two more men burst over the threshold. The last one through the door slammed it shut behind him, a sawn-off shotgun raised in front of his chest.

He panted behind the balaclava mask that covered his face, his voice muffled by the fabric as he leaned against the door.

'Jesus, there're kids here! No one said there'd be kids here!'

The man in the middle, shorter than the other two, spun on his heel to face the younger man. 'Shut the fuck up!'

The boy cried out as the shorter man's feet crushed the robot toy under his foot, then leaned over, grabbed the boy's arm, and dragged him towards the kitchen and the rest of his family.

The ring-leader jerked his eyes away from the boy's father back to the younger man standing by the front door.

'Make sure no one leaves,' he said, and then pointed to the shorter of the three. 'You – put the boy over here next to his Mam.'

The boy cried out as the man who held him changed his grip, forcing him to stand on tiptoe as he stumbled across the linoleum floor to where his mother had collapsed into one of the wooden kitchen chairs, sobbing loudly, her high-pitched wailing filling the room.

The leader jerked his forefinger at the boy's father. 'Shut her up now, or I will.'

His father didn't move, but began to talk. 'Shh, shh, my love. It's okay. It'll be okay.'

His mother's eyes remained wide open as her hysterical sobbing gave way to hiccups as she sucked in air.

His father threw the towel he'd been using onto the draining board next to the sink and turned to face the intruders.

'What the hell do you want?'

To the boy, his father's voice sounded shaky, nervous. He still wore his work clothes – long-sleeved shirt and jeans, heavy steel-capped boots, all covered in dust.

The boy swallowed, one hand on his mother's arm, the other massaging his abdomen as he desperately tried not to pee.

The aroma of roast potatoes and pork chops filled the small space, and the boy's stomach growled, the sound resonating around the kitchen.

In two steps, the intruders' leader had crossed to the boy's father and slapped him hard across his face.

He cried out, setting the boy's mother off on another bout of wailing. The masked man spun on his heel to face her.

'I swear, if you don't shut up, I'll shut you up – permanently,' he hissed.

The boy saw his father's eyes flicker over him and his mother, before he turned and bolted for the back door. His fingers slipped on the key as he turned it, losing precious seconds, and he fumbled with the doorknob in his still-damp hands.

The masked leader reached behind his black sports sweater, pulled out a gun, and dragged the boy's mother from her chair.

'Stop, or I'll shoot her, Barry.'

The man's calm voice resonated through the small space, and the boy flinched, waiting for something terrible to happen, before his father's shoulders slumped.

His father shut the door, its summer-warped surface sticking in the frame for a moment before closing properly. He closed his eyes and rested his palm against the wood and then turned.

The boy felt tears on his cheeks as he saw his father's face. He'd never seen him scared before, and now the man looked petrified.

'I'm so sorry, Pam,' his father whispered. 'I never meant anything to happen to you.' His gaze wavered on the boy, and then focused on the man threatening his family. 'Please, let them go – they've done you no harm.'

The intruders' leader shoved the boy's mother away, and she fell against the kitchen bench, crying out as she knocked her hip against the hard surface.

She pulled the boy to her, knelt down, and gathered him in her arms.

The intruders' leader swung round, punching the boy's father in the stomach and sent him crashing to the ground, before he knelt on the floor next to the man.

He held the back of the man's neck, forcing his face into the linoleum floor, his mouth close to his ear.

'You really thought you could get away with it, didn't you, Barry?' he hissed. 'Did you think you wouldn't get caught? Did you think we wouldn't find you? Now, where is it? Where did you hide it?'

With each question, he banged the man's head against the floor, forcing a grunt from the boy's father with each strike.

The boy forced a wave of nausea back down into his stomach as his father breathed through his mouth, blood from his broken nose dripping onto the tiles.

He whimpered, his eyes fearful as he watched the attack on his father, unable to help him.

Chapter 33

Will stared at Mack, his jaw slack.

Mack chuckled. ‘It’s all starting to come together now, eh, lad?’

Will fell back into his chair. ‘What do you mean? My dad was a building surveyor. He never got involved in anything like that.’

Mack snorted. ‘Bullshit, lad. *Everyone* got involved, one way or another.’ He paused while he lit a cigarette, the flame glowing at the end as he took a long first drag, then blew an elegant smoke ring towards the ceiling before glancing back at Will. ‘Some people just got more involved than others, that’s all.’

‘But the peace accord – it’d been in place for over twelve months by then. Everyone was adhering to the cease fire.’

The older man shook his head. 'Good god. If Barry could hear you now.' Mack pointed a nicotine-stained finger at Will. 'You have no idea what you're talking about. *No idea*.'

He pushed away from the chair, stalked across the room, and stoked the fire.

A loud pop preceded a spark of embers which shot up the chimney, while a light cloud of wood smoke filled the room before the draft caught.

Mack stared at the fireplace, the flames reflected in his eyes, and for a moment, he seemed lost in thought.

Will leaned forward, resting his elbows on his knees, wishing his heart rate would slow down instead of hammering in his ears. 'Then explain it to me,' he said. 'Tell me why a nine-year old boy watched as his dad was beaten in his own kitchen. Tell me why that man disappeared without a trace.' He stood and walked across the room until he was level with the other man. 'Tell me Mack. What on earth did my dad do to deserve that?'

Mack ignored him. He continued to watch the flames in the hearth for what seemed like an age, until he sighed and, leaning forward, extracted the packet of cigarettes and lighter out of his pocket, set them on the mantelpiece, and stared at Will.

'Because he betrayed us.'

'I don't believe you.'

The older man snorted. 'Really? How the hell do you think your dad managed to afford the house you lived in when you were a kid, eh? The new toys you were given, even if it wasn't your birthday or Christmas? The jewellery your ma wore?'

Will rubbed his hand over his face, the images replaying in his mind as Mack spoke, the realisation that his dad had been involved in organised crime, and likely killed for trying to set up one of its leaders, Ian Rossiter.

'Your dad was working for Rossiter on the side, same as the rest of us,' said Mack.

'How successful was he?'

'Put it this way. How the hell do you think Rossiter managed to erase his background and set himself up as the most likely political candidate to win the election? How do you think he paid to create a whole new background for himself, posing as a legitimate successful businessman?' said Mack. He didn't wait for a response. 'Dirty money, that's how.

And he never did his own dirty work,' he added. 'Always had someone do the killing for him. Except one time.'

His eyes met Will's. 'Do you understand what I'm saying, lad? That *one* time he let his temper get the better of him, your Dad was working, out of sight of Rossiter and his men, and realised what was going to happen. He got the only solid evidence that Rossiter is a murderer, and Amy found out about it.'

'Were you there that night? Was it you that took my dad from me?'

Mack fell silent and moved back to his chair, slumping into the cushions with a low grunt. 'No,' he said. 'I wasn't there that night. I was working.' He held up his hand. 'I swear, Will. What Rossiter did to your dad was wrong.'

Will leaned forward, his elbows on his knees, and scratched his ear, trying to process what Mack had told him.

Had his father made the mistake of trying to blackmail Rossiter? Had he simply got greedy? Or had someone betrayed him? And why hadn't Amy shown him the photograph?

'What am I going to do, Mack? Rossiter's already shown what he's capable of. How the hell are we going to stop him?'

'We'll need a plan, lad. We'll work something out, as soon as—'

They both jumped as a key turned in the front door.

'Who's that?' asked Will, his eyes wide. 'Are you expecting someone?'

'Stay here. Keep calm,' said Mack and patted his shoulder. 'I'll be right back.'

He left the room, pulling the door closed, and Will leaned forward, his head in his hands.

Mack's voice reached his ears, muffled, and he strained to hear what was being said. A second voice chimed in, lighter but little more than a murmur.

He gave up, slapped his palms on the armrests, and moved towards the fire place. He crouched, picked up the brass poker and moved the logs around in the grate, more from a need to do something than anything else. He wondered who Mack was talking to, who he'd trust enough to give them a key to his house.

Exhaustion seeped through his body, and he stifled a yawn.

He jerked his head to the side as the door brushed against the carpet and dropped the poker onto the hearth.

'Hello, Will.'

He remained crouched, unable to move, even though he knew his mouth was open.

Erin moved towards Mack's armchair, placed her bag on the floor, and perched on the edge of the cushion, her hands in her lap.

Will's attention snapped back to the door as Mack entered the room. He took one look at Erin, and then seemed to change his mind.

'Maybe you two should talk,' he murmured. 'I'll be out in the kitchen if you need me.'

Mack left and closed the door, leaving the room silent except for the quiet draw of wind in the chimney and the crackle of burning logs.

Erin stared at her fingernails. 'So now you know.'

Will stood, and then moved and kneeled in front of her.

'I'm so sorry, Erin. I had no idea.'

'Why would you?'

'You could have told me, you know.'

She lifted her head, her green eyes boring into him. 'I realise that now.' She sniffled. 'Where does that leave us? What do you want to do?'

Will's heart thumped. He knew exactly what he wanted. He reached out and took her hands in his. 'Now I want to expose Rossiter more than ever.'

He felt the determination soar through him in that moment. Whatever it took, whatever else Ian Rossiter had done, he'd help her.

Relief shone in her eyes. 'Thank you.'

Mack reappeared at the doorway. 'What are you going to do, Will?'

'I'm not sure.' Will stood. 'I need to get back to the motel. Find out if Amy had that photograph anywhere.'

He started as Amy's mobile began to ring from the confines of his backpack. He leaned down, unzipped the bag, and felt sweat break out on his brow when he saw the number.

'I need to take this,' he said, then hurried to the hallway and closed the door. 'Hello?'

'Will – it's Hathaway at the Prince George. How far out of town are you?'

'About an hour.'

'You need to come now, Will. I'm sorry – we're losing her.'

'I'll be right there.'

Will ran back to the front room, Mack following at his heels, worry etched across his face.

Erin rose from her chair as he grabbed his bag. 'What's wrong? What is it?'

'The hospital. Amy's dying. I've got to go.'

A shocked silence followed his words, before they both moved towards him.

'Will, I'm so sorry,' murmured Erin.

'Wait.' said Mack. 'Before you go, you need to take this.'

He shuffled across the room to a beat-up writing bureau, tugged open one of the drawers, and rummaged through the contents until he pulled out an envelope and handed it to him.

Will frowned as he took it from the older man and noticed that his hands were shaking.

'What is it?'

'Just open it.'

Will tore open the envelope and pulled out a thick piece of paper, before he realised it was a photograph.

The back of it was yellow with age and dirty as if it had been hidden somewhere for a long time, perhaps forgotten. His fingers trembled as he turned it in his hands, then he shook his head.

His eyes met Mack's. 'All this time?'

'I had to be sure, Will. I needed to know I could trust you.' Mack moved back to his chair and sat. 'Understand it from my point of view,' he said, jerking his finger at the photograph. 'That was my only insurance. My only way of staying alive.'

Will ran his palm over the image, a bead of sweat working its way down his forehead as the implication of what he held sank in.

His father had caught the exact moment the bullet had entered the man's skull, Rossiter's arm still outstretched, holding the murder weapon. A spray of blood held in the air above the victim's head as his body jerked backwards, caught in time.

And Mack stood to one side of Rossiter, a gun in his hand, his face grim.

'Will? Are you okay?'

Erin's voice cut through his thoughts, her tone concerned as she sat down next to him and leaned across to look at the photograph. She recoiled when she saw what it depicted.

'Oh my god.'

'I'm sorry, love,' said Mack. 'But you knew I wasn't a good man.'

He moved and placed an arm around his daughter's shoulders. 'This is my way of trying to put something right. Please understand.'

'Where did you get this?' Will said, still staring at the image.

'Your father,' he said. 'He told me not to open the envelope or give it to anyone else but you. He asked me to look after it for him, in case anything happened.'

Will exhaled, rubbing the shiny aged surface under his thumbs. 'Why didn't you tell me sooner? All this time…'

'I needed to know if you were serious about stopping him,' said Mack. 'I needed to know if you were going to help Erin.'

Will stood, pacing the small room, the photograph in his hands.

Now, everything made sense.

Why Rossiter was so desperate to cover his tracks. Why Amy had so doggedly pursued the story for so long. Why Rossiter was willing to kill anyone who tried to stop him. Why none of it would end until the political candidate's history had been exposed.

Why the truth had to be told.

About everything.

Chapter 34

Mack had hugged his daughter before ushering her out his front door after Will.

'Stay with him,' he urged. 'It's too dangerous to be near me now. Rossiter will hunt me down, for sure.'

'What are you going to do?'

She grasped hold of his wrist, and he gently peeled her fingers away from his sleeve, then kissed her hand.

'I'll think of something,' he said. 'But you need to go. Rossiter's going to be looking for all of us.'

'But where do I go?' Erin had looked from him to Will, her expression bewildered. 'I can't go to the hospital – it wouldn't be right.'

I'll take you back to the motel,' said Will, and then caught the older man's gaze. 'It's on the way.'

Mack had nodded, watched the pair of them hurry down the short garden path away from him, and had then closed the door before Erin had the chance to turn and see the tears that streaked his cheeks.

He hurried through to the kitchen, wiping at his eyes with the sleeve of his cardigan.

He opened a cupboard door and rummaged amongst the jars of pasta sauce and tins of food until he found a shallow box. Flipping open the lid, he pulled out a pair of the latex catering gloves, tossed the box back into the cupboard, and slipped the gloves over his hands.

He dragged one of the dining chairs across the linoleum floor until it was next to the kitchen cupboards, then climbed up onto the padded seat, placed a hand on one of the cupboard doors to steady himself and reached up, his fingers working along the gap between the top of the cabinet and the ceiling.

His brow creased, then he grunted as he found what he was looking for.

He dragged the bundle of rags to the edge of the cupboard, then grabbed it in his fist and stepped down. Turning, he set the bundle on the kitchen table and unwrapped it.

The gun was over twenty years old, but gleamed under the fluorescent lights.

His thoughts turned to Will, and the fact that the man had been led here all along by Amy, solely for the purpose of exposing the politician for what he really was. He wondered if the journalist had known about Will's past, or had uncovered it while investigating Erin's accusations.

His gaze shifted to the calendar on the wall, the election date of May seventh circled with the thick line from a felt permanent marker pen.

Why now? Will had asked.

'Why not?' Mack had asked flippantly.

The reality was, once Erin had told him the truth, once he knew the suffering Rossiter had caused her since she was seven years old, his days were numbered.

The significance of the election date and Erin's age when Rossiter had first made her endure his sickening habits had not been lost on either of them.

In fact, it was what had driven them, then Amy, to wreck Rossiter's career once and for all.

Except Mack had to be sure.

He trusted Will, had grown to like him even before he'd met him, thanks to Amy – who seemed to know more about Will's past than the man himself had been happy to admit.

She'd been thorough, for sure. Although he felt bad that Amy's survival was unlikely, he was pleased to see the effect Will had on Erin.

He picked up the revolver. At least he'd be leaving her in safe hands.

He pulled open a drawer built under the table and grasped a small cardboard box fixed to the back of it.

Setting it on the table, he slid the box open and tapped six of its brass contents into his palm.

The thirty-two calibre rounds were small, but effective.

Mack tipped open the revolver and methodically pushed each of the rounds into its individual chamber.

When he was done, he re-wrapped the gun in its cloths, put six more rounds in the pocket of his cardigan, and swept his car keys from the china dish on the window sill.

He paused next to the back door for a heartbeat, then hurried through the back garden, through a gate in the fence, and made his way to the lock-up that housed his old two-door hatchback.

He trusted Will, but he had to be sure.

One way or another, Ian Rossiter wouldn't be elected Prime Minister next week.

***

Mack had pulled his small car to the side of the road after leaving the motorway and had paged through his battered old road atlas until he'd found Rossiter's house.

Newer maps would omit the ministerial candidate's home for security purposes but Mack's version was already a decade old and still clearly marked the location of the property, its heritage listing punctuated by a blue icon next to its name.

He traced his finger over the lanes around the perimeter, found one within walking distance of the house, and half an hour later had parked on its verge.

The car held no indication of its owner's identity to a would-be thief – the glove compartment was empty, no litter filled the back seats, and the ancient CD player had been torn from its housing before Mack had taken delivery of the vehicle.

In short, it would need a police officer with access to the UK vehicle registration database to work out who the vehicle belonged to, which was exactly what Mack wanted.

If anything went wrong, he wanted the police to knock on Rossiter's door.

Mack reached into his back pocket and wiggled the latex gloves over his fingers once more. He'd removed them while driving, not wanting to arouse immediate suspicion if the police had pulled him over during his journey. Now, his hands covered once more, he opened the back door of the car and felt around under the seat until he located the concealed gun.

He climbed out, locked the doors, and began the short trek to the electric gates that led to the house.

He'd seen the news, and Will had confirmed what he'd gleaned from the television – following the attack, Rossiter announced he'd be spending the remainder of the election campaign working from home.

He's got his back to the wall, thought Mack.

Which meant that Rossiter wasn't convinced that Gregory had the situation completely under control.

And, until Will announced it, Rossiter wouldn't find out about Amy's rapidly deteriorating health until it was too late.

Although unspoken between them, they both knew it changed everything. Now, the tables were turned, and they were in control. As long as Will remained alive long enough to expose the corrupt businessman.

As he neared the gate, he adjusted his cardigan to camouflage the bulge of the gun and cracked his knuckles.

Mack checked over his shoulder. The lane was deserted in both directions, devoid of any traffic noise.

Satisfied, he adjusted the gun in his waistband, then removed the gloves, bundled them together, and tossed them into the undergrowth at the side of the road.

The sun had begun its descent over the horizon, its last rays flickering behind the grey clouds that had threatened more rain all day. Leaf litter stuck to the soles of his shoes as he walked along the lane towards his destination, and he felt the cool spring air begin to seep into his joints.

He began to cough, and stopped, leaning over with his hands on his knees until the spasm passed. He hawked the contents of his mouth into the undergrowth, ignored the now familiar pink tinge, and instead picked up his pace.

Approaching the entrance to the driveway that led up to the house, he gazed up at the enormous wrought-iron gates that loomed over him, two concrete pillars supporting their weight. They were closed, but Mack couldn't see a chain around them.

He moved his head and saw the security panel set into the right-hand pillar, then raised his eyes to the camera perched at the top of the pillar, a red light blinking on its surface.

Mack threw a mock salute at it, then stepped forward and pressed the intercom button with the knuckle of his index finger.

A man's voice answered, no doubt the same man who was monitoring the live feed from the camera.

'Identify yourself, and state the purpose of your visit.'

A sly smile began to twitch at the corner of Mack's mouth, and he turned away from the camera so the security man wouldn't see.

'Mackenzie Harris,' he said, bending down to the microphone to make sure the man at the other end of the line would hear him clearly. 'Tell your boss and his creep of a press secretary that the ghost of Christmas past is here to see them.'

***

Mack had been waiting at the gates for almost ten minutes before he heard a metallic click and the ironwork began to swing inwards on its hinges.

Impatient, he slid between them as soon as the gap was big enough to accommodate him and began to walk up the driveway, his feet crunching on the gravel beneath his shoes.

He half expected to be apprehended by Rossiter's thugs halfway up the driveway when he reached a small copse of trees, but the landscape remained still, save for the evening singsong of a blackbird.

He stood for a moment, entranced by the sound, aware that it could well be the last time he heard the beautiful melody. He shook his head as, beyond the trees, another bird echoed the song, and then he adjusted his waistband to counteract the weight of the gun, recalling the last time it had been fired.

A grim determination seized him, and he took a deep breath before striding towards the house.

Will might have the photographic evidence now, but the lad needed a push in the right direction if Rossiter was going to be stopped.

Mack's mind turned to the image of the calendar on his kitchen wall. The election was less than a week away, and the news coverage had reached fever pitch.

Rossiter wouldn't stay holed up at his house forever, Mack was sure. At some point, he'd have to work the crowds face-to-face, to drive the frenzy to his advantage.

It had to be now or never.

The driveway opened out into a large turning circle in front of the house.

Mack stared at the towering gables, trying to recall when he had last been at the property, then quickly dismissed the thought, the memory too painful given what he'd learned from Erin in recent months.

The front door was already open, a large man in a private security uniform standing on the threshold, glaring at him. He moved to one side to let Mack pass, and then slammed the door shut.

Mack had no time to react as a second man emerged from the shadows and shoved him against the wall. Instead, he concentrated on keeping his breathing shallow, despite his racing heartbeat, while the man frisked him.

It took seconds for the revolver to be discovered, the extra rounds moments later.

'What have you got?'

Even after all the years that had passed, the voice still managed to fill Mack with dread.

He turned his head.

Rossiter stood, silhouetted in a doorway off the hallway, lamplight glowing from the room beyond to ward off the failing light from outside. His arms were crossed over his chest, his legs slightly apart.

He cast an imposing figure, and Mack inwardly cursed at the cancer that had weakened his own body.

The security guard kept one hand on Mack's shoulder and passed the gun to his colleague, who strode across to where Rossiter stood.

He reached out and took the gun from the man and turned it over in his hands.

A second man stepped into the doorway from inside the room, a crystal glass held delicately between his fingers.

'Well, well,' said Gregory. 'Look what the cat dragged in.'

'Tell your men to stop searching for Will Fletcher and my niece,' said Rossiter, his eyes gleaming. 'I've thought of a way we can make them come to us.'

Mack turned his face back to the wall and closed his eyes.

He knew what would happen next.

Chapter 35

Will steered the car into the first available space, grabbed his backpack from the seat beside him, and then tore across the car park towards the hospital entrance.

The foyer was busy, crowded with the sick and injured pouring in from the city night, a pungent smell of sweat, blood, and fear crawling up the walls. The nurse's station along one side was three-deep with people, a mixture of harried-looking police officers, parents with children in their arms, worried families, and surly drunks.

He dodged around a porter pushing an elderly woman in a wheelchair, a patch covering her eyebrow and bruises on her cheek, and ran to the end of the corridor.

He punched the button for the elevator and paced impatiently. He was debating whether to take the stairs when the doors finally opened. Tempted to drag its occupants from the car, he stood to one side to let them pass, then barrelled into the elevator and hit the button for Amy's ward, then the button to close the doors, apologising under his breath to the porter and his charge who arrived too late and glared at him through the closing gap.

His throat dry, he replayed the short conversation he'd had with her surgeon in his mind. The man hadn't elaborated further, only reiterating that Will should hurry.

He turned his back to the doors, wrapped his fingers round the brass railing that encircled the elevator space, and stared at his reflection in the mirrored wall.

Dark circles pooled under his eyelids, his eyes red and sore. He rubbed a hand across his chin, feeling the stubble that prickled his skin, and tried to remember when he'd last shaved. His hair stood on end, and as the elevator travelled farther upwards through the guts of the hospital, he ran his hand through it and tried to slick it into place.

It looked worse.

He spun round at the sound of a soft *ping* and burst through the doors as they opened, then skidded across the tiled floor, and came to a halt next to the ward nurse's desk.

She held a phone to her ear and held up a hand to stop Will from interrupting. She spoke softly, succinctly, issuing instructions, taking notes, until finally she finished the call and put the receiver down.

'Yes? What can I do for you?'

'I'm here about Amy Peters,' said Will. 'Mr Hathaway phoned me earlier. He told me to get here as soon as possible.'

Will gulped, out of breath, both from the rush to the ward from the car park and the sheer panic that wound across his chest.

The woman pursed her lips. 'I'll let him know you're here.'

She gestured to a seat while she picked up the phone again, but Will ignored her.

He couldn't sit still, not now.

Dread began to seize him, worming its way into his mind as the seconds drew out. The soft tones of the nurse's voice reached him, but despite holding his breath and standing still, pretending to look at a poster on the wall, he couldn't hear what was being said.

The phone was returned to its cradle, and the corridor returned to the steady beat of a busy ward, the far-off sounds of machines beeping, patients moaning, and calm, soothing voices.

At the sound of footsteps echoing off the walls towards him, Will turned and knew before the surgeon even reached him what his words would be.

He could see it in the man's face, the look of defeat, exhaustion, and sorrow etching lines across the man's features. Yet he said nothing, not until Hathaway reached out and took him by the arm.

'Thanks for coming so quickly, Will,' he murmured. 'Let's go through to this room here, shall we?'

He opened a door and led Will through to a small office which had been stripped bare of any official hospital paraphernalia and instead had been laid out with a decor the interior designer probably marketed as calming.

Two green armchairs sat at angles facing each other, a soft plush material that looked a little threadbare on closer inspection. A square white coffee table had been planted between the chairs while, next to the window, a dark green fern fought to escape the pot it had been squashed into.

Will tore his eyes away from the silvery spider web that wrapped around two of the leaves and turned his attention back to Hathaway, who was trying to usher him into one of the armchairs. He acquiesced, dropped the backpack to his feet, and waited, his hands folded in his lap.

'Will, I'm very sorry. We did everything we possibly could,' Hathaway began, his eyes searching Will's face. 'I'm sorry to have to tell you that Amy passed away thirty minutes ago.'

Will felt the rush of air leave his lungs as he leaned forward on his knees and wrapped his hands around his head. He stared at the mottled grey and green carpet, his chest tightening as a deep primitive ache began to encircle his chest.

'I thought she was going to be okay,' he whispered. 'I thought…'

'Her injuries were too great,' said the surgeon. 'Trauma to the head is always very, very difficult to treat. We did our best, and I'm satisfied my team couldn't have done any more.'

'Did she… would she have felt it?'

'She died peacefully, Will. She wasn't in any pain. She'd been heavily sedated since coming out of surgery,' said Hathaway. 'She simply slipped away from us.'

Will lifted his head as the surgeon finished speaking, his eyes stinging, and then he dry-heaved.

Hathaway kicked the wastepaper bin across the floor, and Will grabbed it, his stomach contracting painfully from lack of food. Bile stung the back of his throat, and he retched.

The surgeon moved across the room and placed a comforting hand on Will's shoulders until the tremors subsided, before taking the container away from him and placing it near the door.

Will leaned back, his nostrils flaring at the putrid stench, and with shaking hands, he took the glass of water the surgeon had held out to him.

He nodded his thanks, and guzzled half the water, his eyes stinging with tears.

Hathaway pushed a box of paper tissues towards him, and he took two, shoving one in his pocket and gripping the other in his hand.

He panted as he tried to fight down the urge to be sick once more, and sipped the remaining water.

'Could you keep this quiet for a while, to give me time to let our friends know before they hear about it on breakfast news or something?'

'Of course. I'll ask the police to do the same.'

Will sniffled. 'I want to see her.'

'Of course.'

He followed Hathaway from the room, avoiding the nurse's gaze as they passed the reception counter for the ward, and continued past her to a second corridor that led farther into the bowels of the hospital. After a few paces, the surgeon stood to one side and pushed open a door.

'This is the chapel of rest,' he said, then placed a hand on Will's shoulder. 'Take as long as you need. I'll be outside.'

Will nodded, sniffled, then stepped inside.

The room had been painted and furnished in a non-denominational decor, with three short rows of seats on each side of a central aisle. Soft lighting pooled around the space from wall sconces, casting shadows amongst the large picture frames that held photographs of landscape scenes.

Will stuffed his hands in his pockets and walked slowly forward, his fingernails digging into his palms.

His footsteps were soundless on the thick burgundy carpet, and he realised the walls must have been sound-proofed, as the noise from the hospital had fallen silent as the door closed behind him, cocooning him in the space.

He reached the front row of chairs and exhaled.

In front of him, a simple open casket had been laid out on a raised altar, a figure visible within the folds of material that lined it.

He sank into the chair nearest to him and rested his head in his hands.

A memory resurfaced, unwanted, of him sitting next to his mother, several years ago now, after she'd fought long and hard with the authorities to have her husband declared dead, so they could try to move on with their lives.

They'd sat in a room, like this, alone except for an embarrassed funeral director and a ticking clock, staring at a casket they knew to be empty, while the man standing in front of them intoned the eulogy.

The service had been brutally short. His mother's illness had spiralled not long afterwards.

Guilt consumed Will as he wondered what he would have done differently, if he could have that last morning with Amy back.

Would she have agreed to meet Rossiter at the hotel alone again, knowing her life was in danger? What if it was sunny, instead of raining? Would she have accepted Rossiter's offer of a lift in his car?

He shook his head, trying to clear the thoughts, knowing full well he would be dragged down into a depression from which there would be no escape this time.

Standing on shaking legs, he moved towards the casket, not sure what he would find.

The surgeon's team had been kind. They had cleaned Amy's face, wrapped a thin blue towel around her head, hiding the scars of surgery. A sheet had been pulled up over her body, the same colour as the towel.

Will reached out and fingered the material. It matched her eyes perfectly, but he'd never see them again. She looked as if she was asleep, her face impassive, her hands folded across her chest, her face paler than he could ever remember.

He leaned forward and kissed her cool unmoving cheek, before touching her face, his fingers tracing her jawline as tears splashed onto the sheet.

'Sleep well, Amy,' he murmured, his voice shaking. 'You're safe now.'

Chapter 36

Will pulled into the car park of the motel, switched off the engine, and leaned his head on the steering wheel.

He couldn't recall the drive from London. His movements had been automatic, reacting to road signs and the traffic in a trance, all the while thinking of Amy.

He'd held out his hands for the bag a nurse handed to him while Amy's surgeon had spoken to him, before he peered inside and realised it was the remainder of Amy's clothing, minus her blood-stained suit jacket and blouse. Those had been taken by the police.

His throat ached from holding back the tears, afraid that if he started, he wouldn't stop and would have to pull the car over to the side of the road.

Instead, he needed to run, to go back to the motel and hide from the world, to mourn.

As Hathaway had coaxed him through the forms that had to be signed, the man had spoken of funeral arrangements, counselling services, and solicitors, but the words had washed over Will.

He leaned back and opened his eyes. Soon, he knew he'd have to deal with all of that. For the moment, though, he wanted to stay away from it all, the reality of having to continue without Amy almost too much to bear.

His fingers found the door release, and he stepped out into the cold night air. He slipped his backpack over his shoulder, locked the car, and stalked across the car park, the muted lights from the motel rooms chasing his shadow across the asphalt.

Walking along the corridor towards his room, he fished into his pocket for his key card, then froze, conscious of movement behind the door, a shadow moving in the light that streamed from under the threshold.

Erin tore it open, her face distraught.

'You're here,' she whispered and grabbed his hand, pulling him into the room.

Will let the backpack slide to the floor as she ran her fingers over his cheeks, tracing the tears that now flowed.

'I'm sorry,' she said. 'I'm so, so sorry.'

She pulled him to the small sofa and sat with him, cradling his head on her shoulder as he wept, his whole body shaking with the grief that wracked him.

Somehow, he'd thought Amy would survive. She'd always been the tougher of the two of them, no matter what life threw at her. She'd simply pick herself up, dust herself down, and return stronger. Except this time, Rossiter had well and truly broken her.

'What am I going to do?' he whispered.

'We'll figure something out,' soothed Erin, stroking his hair. She pressed her lips to his forehead. 'We'll find a way.'

'He's too powerful.'

'We'll find a way.'

Will sniffled and eased away from Erin. 'I should check my messages,' he said. 'I didn't get a chance at the hospital.'

He pulled the phone out of his bag, inserted the battery, and a new message icon blinked on the screen. He dialled his voicemail service, and then frowned as the female voice told him the message was from a withheld number.

He nearly dropped the phone when the message began.

'It's him.'

'Put it on speaker.' Erin drew her knees up to her chin and wrapped her arms around her legs. 'I want to hear it.'

Will laid the phone on the dresser and pressed the 'play' option on the display.

The voice of the likely heir to the Parliamentary throne filled the room, his haughty tone belying his rough origins.

'Well, well, well,' he said. 'You *have* been busy, Billy Fletcher, haven't you? Come a long way since your dad disappeared, eh?'

Will dug his fingernails into his palms as he paced the room.

'Now, listen to me, Billy.' Rossiter's voice lowered to a dangerous pitch. 'I'm sorry about Amy. I really am, but she was sticking her nose in places she shouldn't have been. Maybe I can get her some specialist help, depending on how well you assist me.'

He paused, and Will imagined the man shrugging as he delivered his condolences, before continuing.

'And now I have the same problem with you.' There was another pause, and the sound of a glass being moved on a table. 'Except you've been smart, Billy. I don't know where to find you. And you have my niece with you. Lovely piece of skin, isn't she?'

Erin jumped up from the sofa and covered her mouth with her hand, before moving to the window and stared out into the night.

Will focussed on the phone, and the voice that consumed him.

'So, what's a man to do, Billy, eh? I'll tell you what he does. Listen to this.'

Will heard a scrambling sound on the line, muffled voices, and then Mack's voice rang out.

'Don't pay any attention to him, Will! You get that information to the right people—' His voice cut into an agonised scream.

Will leapt forward and turned the volume down on the phone, his insides curdling.

Mack's scream subsided to a sob, and Rossiter returned to the phone.

'Did you hear that, Billy? Did you hear him scream?' he said. 'Want to know something? Your dad screamed louder than that when I got my hands on him.'

'Yeah, but he kept his mouth shut about his secret!' Mack shouted in the background. 'He was a hero, Will!'

There was a grunt, and Mack fell silent again.

'He wasn't a hero,' hissed Rossiter. 'He was a lying bastard. Same as you, Mack.'

The elderly man screamed in the background, and Erin let out a sob, before running to the bathroom. The sound of her vomiting reached Will's ears as he picked up the phone.

Rossiter cleared his throat. 'Now, Billy, this is what you're going to do. You're going to bring all the information you've got on me, including the hard drive – I'm presuming the bitch had another one – and the photograph. You get it to me before nine o'clock tomorrow morning, or Mack dies. If he dies, it's because of you,' he continued. 'And if he dies, then you and Erin are next. Don't fuck about, Will. There are no second chances.'

Will switched the phone off and threw it onto the bed, before leaning against the wall and sinking to the floor, his legs shaking.

The bathroom door opened, and Erin appeared, her face pale.

'He means it, doesn't he?'

Will nodded, his head tilted back as he stared at the ceiling. 'I can't let him torture Mack,' he said. 'I can't. This has to end.'

Erin sank onto the bed and leaned her elbows on her knees. 'We can't let him win,' she said. 'We have to do something.'

'You heard him. Nine o'clock tomorrow morning.' Will checked his watch. 'It's ten o'clock now. We've got eleven hours to hand everything over.'

'Surely there's a way?' Anguish creased Erin's brow. 'Even if you hand over the photograph and all the files, Will, he'll destroy us both, don't you see? This will *never* end.'

Will rubbed his hand across his eyes and got to his feet. He ran his fingers through Erin's hair, her green eyes red-rimmed, pleading with him.

As Erin's voice fell silent, Will's mind began to work.

He wiped his sleeve across his eyes and tried to concentrate, his thoughts jumbled up with his grief.

Then it hit him.

With Amy dead, Rossiter no longer had a way to blackmail him. Maybe it was time to turn the tables.

His heart lurched as another thought began to go round in his head.

Rossiter didn't know Amy had died. If he had, he'd never have risked leaving such a voicemail message.

Will's gaze fell to the external hard drive plugged into the laptop, its single green light blinking on the side of its black surface.

What Amy had uncovered was volatile; the hard drive on the desk was a bomb waiting to explode. All he had to do now was set the timer.

He chewed his lip, then reached across and switched his phone back on.

If Rossiter was going to play dirty, then it was time to raise the stakes.

The number he wanted was already in the recent calls list.

'Kirby? If I drive to your offices right now with an exclusive story about Ian Rossiter, how soon are you able to print it?'

Chapter 37

'Okay, Will. What's this all about?'

Kirby Clark closed the conference room door and gestured to an empty seat.

Will lowered himself into the chair and hugged his backpack to his chest. 'Who are all these people?'

'To your left, Mike Tate, who's our in-house counsel, Stephen Reeves, our operations manager, and Jeannette Ryder, one of our senior political journalists. Jeanette works with Amy, but they follow their own leads. I think she'll be the best one to help us with this, given her background in following the UK political climate on a regular basis.'

Will shook hands with each person as they leaned across the desk to him.

Kirby raised an eyebrow. 'Well?'

'It's about the story Amy was working on,' said Will. 'And the reason why she was targeted in the attack on Ian Rossiter's car earlier this week.'

A hush fell on the room as four people stared at him, in varying states of shock.

'Go on,' said Mike eventually.

Jeanette opened her notebook to a fresh page, popped the lid off her pen, and began to write.

Will unzipped his backpack, pulled out the hard drive, his notes, and his mother's bible and took a deep breath. 'Amy was shot by people employed by Rossiter to silence her,' he said.

'Why?'

'Because she had evidence to support her theory that Rossiter was directly involved with an organised criminal gang in Belfast between 1999 and 2000,' he said.

He went on to explain the events of the past few days, through returning to the flat to find it ransacked, then discovering Simon's death. He told them about his theory concerning the hit and run accident involving Russell.

'He's silencing everyone that ever came into contact with this information,' he said.

'Will, this is all very well,' said Kirby, 'and of course we'd like to take a look at that hard drive with you to see what Amy discovered, but,' he held up his hand to stop Will interrupting, 'so far, what you're telling us is all circumstantial. Do you have any hard evidence that Rossiter was involved in a criminal gang?'

'Try this.' Will slipped the photograph from where he'd tucked it between the pages of the bible and slid it across the table, keeping his fingers pressed to the corner.

He watched as Mike's Adam's apple bobbed in his throat.

'Where the hell did you get this?' he demanded. 'Are there copies?'

Will shook his head. 'This is the only one. You'll understand if I insist that it doesn't leave my sight.'

Kirby leaned forward. 'All right. You've got us interested. What else do you have? Why am I at work at one o'clock in the morning?'

Will pulled the photograph back towards him. 'Rossiter has a friend of mine held captive. I think at his house. Unless I hand over everything you see here before nine o'clock this morning, he'll kill him. Just like everyone else.' He raised his eyes to Kirby. 'And then he's going to kill me.'

He lowered his gaze to the photograph between his hands. 'I figured if I could persuade you to publish the truth – what he's done – before the deadline, then Rossiter will be exposed for what he really is. And maybe my friend will be safe.'

'Why come here first?' Why not go straight to the police?' asked Mike. He waved at the papers Will had spread out on the table. 'You've got some compelling evidence here.'

'I don't know if I can trust the police,' said Will. 'Through all of this, Rossiter's managed to keep up with me, tracking my movements.' He looked around the table at the faces staring at him. 'How has he managed to do that if he hasn't got help on the inside?'

'Are you sure this isn't a personal vendetta?' Mike swung his chair round and stood, pacing the length of the room. 'Your girlfriend's in a coma, and two of your friends have been killed. Isn't this just your way of circumventing the justice system to go after Rossiter?'

Will folded his arms and leaned back in his chair. 'If you don't want the story, say so. I'll go to the *Guardian* or something instead.'

Kirby held up his hand. 'We didn't say we don't want the story,' he said. 'Mike has to make sure that you're not bringing this to us to simply seek revenge on Rossiter. We need to know what your intentions are.'

Will snorted. 'My intentions? How about bringing a corrupt businessman to justice for what he's done to people before he becomes our next Prime Minister? Is that enough justification for you?'

The room fell silent.

Mike gestured to Kirby and the two men stepped out of the room, closing the door.

Will watched through the frosted glass as they talked, then he began to gather the photographs, news cuttings, and his mother's bible off the table and stuff them into his backpack. As he zipped up the bag, the door re-opened. Kirby stood to one side to let Mike into the room, and then sat.

'All right, Will,' he said. 'Mike's agreed to let us go ahead and write the story.' He turned to the senior reporter. 'Jeanette – I need you to sit with him, punch this out as quickly as you can.' He glanced at his watch. 'I need you to have this ready for review within the hour, okay?'

The woman nodded and flipped open her laptop computer. 'No problem.'

'Stephen – come with me. I need to go over the layouts for the morning edition, see what we can pull out to fit this in.'

'Okay,' said Jeanette, as silence returned to the room. 'Let's start at the beginning. From when you saw the news report. You talk, I'll type, and I'll tell you if you need to slow down or clarify anything. Sound good?'

'Sure.' Will reached across the table, filled two glasses with water, and passed one across to the reporter. He took a sip, and then began.

As he spoke, she peppered him with questions – why did Amy go ahead with the interview if she believed her life was in danger? How did she trace Rossiter? Where did she find the photograph? On and on until Will had told her the story several times, from several angles, until she was happy.

Will rubbed his eyes and stifled a yawn as Jeannette finished typing her report.

The water jug stood in the middle of the table, empty, and he drained the last of the contents in his glass. His throat hoarse, he realised he'd have to go through it all again with the police, and glanced at his watch.

'Now what happens?' he asked as Jeannette emitted a sigh and closed the laptop.

'Kirby will read through it, make any changes he wants to, then it'll go to Mike. He'll check it for any contentious issues – anything that could land us with a libel case if we printed it. Once they're both happy, it'll go to print.'

Will moved to the window, stretching his back.

Across the cityscape, people slept, oblivious to what he'd been through for the past four days. He traced the bright lights that shone through the cold air beyond the glass, before he leaned his forehead against the pane as his eyes found the illuminated London Eye, the huge wheel dormant and waiting for its paying public to return.

On the opposite bank of the river, the Palace of Westminster loomed out of the metropolis, and he wondered what it would be like to be in the building when the newspaper story went public in a few hours' time.

He jerked away from the glass at the sound of the door handle turning, and Kirby's team walked back in.

Jeanette wore a pensive expression, her eyes tired from the evening's activities. While Mike sat down, she leaned against the wall of the conference room, nibbling a fingernail.

Will caught Kirby's eye and raised an eyebrow. 'Well?'

The older man nodded. 'It's good, Will. But Mike has to check it yet. Let him read it through, and then he can let us know.'

He turned as Stephen joined them, a tray of coffee in his hands. 'Thought everyone might appreciate this,' he said and placed it on the table.

As one, the team launched themselves at the steaming mugs, adding copious amounts of sugar and milk before returning to their seats.

The aroma of freshly ground beans struck Will's senses, and his stomach rumbled. He tried to remember when he'd last eaten, then dismissed the thought. He'd have time to eat when this was all over.

Will drummed his fingers on the desk as Mike read through the report, his heartbeat loud in his ears. He glanced down at a light touch on the back of his hand.

'Keep still,' said Jeannette. 'Let him concentrate.'

After another ten minutes, Mike removed his reading glasses and placed them on the document in front of him.

'Well?' said Kirby. 'What do you think?'

'I think you've got a story,' said Mike. He held up his hand as Will exhaled and leaned back in his chair. 'The police aren't going to be happy about it, but the phrasing is such that it won't land us in court.'

He pushed the paperwork across the table to Will, who grabbed them and began to read.

His brow furrowed. 'Hang on,' he said, holding the pages in the air. 'This isn't all of it.'

'That's the printable part,' said Mike. 'Once the story breaks, we can start to release the rest of it.'

'But…'

'Will,' said Kirby, 'this is the way it has to be. If you want us to help you, we have to do it like this. Otherwise, Rossiter will sue us and no one will ever hear your story.'

'But he'll come up with excuses,' said Will. 'He'll deny everything.'

Mike shook his head. 'Not unless he wants to be charged with perjury,' he said and pointed at the envelope next to Will's hand. 'That photograph is irrefutable evidence. If he does deny what we print this morning, he's going to look an idiot by the time we're finished with him.'

'A dangerous idiot,' said Will.

Mike shrugged, but remained silent.

'Okay,' said Kirby. 'Mike, to confirm – you're happy for us to go to print with this now?'

The legal counsel nodded and began to pack up his notebooks. 'I am. I'll be in my office if you need me for anything,' he said as he moved towards the door. 'I have a feeling we're going to be in for a busy day.'

Jeanette gathered up the pages Will had scattered across the desk. 'Good luck, Will,' she said, then followed Stephen out the conference room, the operations manager already on his mobile phone, barking orders to the printers.

'What will you do now?' asked Kirby.

Will put his empty coffee mug onto the boardroom table, picked up his backpack, and turned towards the door. He glanced over his shoulder.

'How long have I got?'

The editor looked at his watch. 'The printing will be finished in two hours,' he said. 'We'll publish on the online version the moment the papers are distributed.'

'How long, Kirby?'

The older man sighed. 'I can give you four hours.'

'Then I'd better be going.'

'Good luck.' Kirby held out his hand.

'Thanks,' said Will. 'I think I'm going to need it.'

Chapter 38

Will concentrated on his breathing, fighting to stay calm.

He'd pulled DCI Lake's business card from his pocket as soon as he'd returned to the motel and told Erin his plan, and now he sat on the end of the bed while the dial tone buzzed in his ear.

'He'll be asleep,' said Erin, who had perched on the edge of the desk, her hands gripping the surface.

'I know.'

'What are you going to tell him?'

'Enough that he'll know I'm serious,' said Will. 'Is the email ready?'

'Yes.'

She moved out of the way so that Will could see the laptop computer and the email that they'd drafted together over the past half an hour, with a single file attached.

'Okay. Here goes.'

Will hit the 'send' button on the phone and it chirped in his ear as it dialled the number and then began to ring.

He was hoping the policeman would keep his mobile phone next to his bed during such a high profile case, and he wasn't disappointed when a sleepy voice answered.

'DCI Lake. Speak.'

'It's Will Fletcher.'

'Will?' There was a moment's pause, a shuffling at the other end of the line, and then the policeman's voice returned, a little clearer. 'It's three o'clock in the morning. What do you want?'

Will's insides twisted as he wondered whether it had been a good idea to phone the detective at home. The man didn't sound like he had had much sleep.

'Do you have access to a computer there?'

'Yes. Why?'

'Go and switch it on.'

Will waited while the detective cursed under his breath, and then heard him mumble something to his wife.

Her reply was muffled, but her tone terse.

Will heard the other man walking through his house, before a door squeaked on its hinges and a light switch was pressed.

'All right, Will,' said Lake. He exhaled as a chair creaked under his weight and a computer beeped to life. 'It's three in the morning. I haven't even had time for a coffee. You've been impossible to contact, and then you phone me in the middle of the night? What do you want? What the hell's going on?'

'Check your emails.'

Will turned and nodded to Erin, who reached over and tapped the 'send' button on the screen.

At the other end of the line, Lake started up his email programme, the light touch of his fingers on the keys filtering down the line.

'I presume you want me to open this?'

'Yes. Tell me when you've downloaded the attachment, too.'

'Okay. Done.'

'All right. Bear with me. This is going to take a bit of time.'

'This had better be good,' the detective growled.

Will took a deep breath, and then began.

When he had finished, the detective remained silent, until Will could bear it no more.

'Are you still there?'

'Shut up a minute. I'm taking some notes.'

Will bit his lip and waited while the silence dragged out. Erin held up her hands, her head tilted to one side. He shrugged, and then held up his hand as the detective returned to the phone.

'It'll take me some time to look into this,' he said. 'I need to corroborate the evidence before I can do anything else.'

Will glanced at his watch. 'You've got three hours,' he said.

The policeman hissed through his teeth. 'You're not in a position to make demands,' he said.

'In three hours, Amy's editor is going to print this story,' said Will. 'He has the original photograph.'

He heard a loud *bang* at the other end of the line and realised Lake had kicked a filing cabinet.

'What the hell?'

'I needed some insurance. In case you didn't take me seriously.'

'You put me in a difficult position.'

'That was the idea.'

'I could have you arrested.'

'I'm aware of that.'

'Stay near the phone.'

The line went dead, and Will lowered his mobile to his lap.

'What did he say?' asked Erin, her voice breathless. 'Is he going to help us?'

'I hope so,' said Will. 'Otherwise we're really in the shit.'

Chapter 39

Will reached out and squeezed Erin's hand, her fingers cold under his touch.

When he'd first parked the rental car and switched off the engine and lights, their breath had fogged up the windscreen. In the darkness of the lane, damp air had slowly seeped into the vehicle.

They'd passed an abandoned vehicle a mile away, and Erin had cried out in surprise, before explaining it belonged to Mack.

Will had shaken his head. 'That means they didn't find him.'

They had stared at each other in shock.

'He went to them,' exclaimed Erin. 'Why would he be so stupid?' She'd bashed her fist against the upholstery of the car while tears coursed down her cheeks. 'He must've known what they'd do to him.'

All Will could do was hold her while she sobbed.

Now, his whole body ached with its attempts to keep warm, despite the extra layers of clothing he'd thrown on. He glanced sideways at Erin as he felt a shiver move through her body under his touch.

'How long do you think they'll be?'

'I don't know. It's been an hour,' he said. 'They can't be far away.'

'Do you think he believed you?'

'Yes.'

'What makes you so sure?' She twisted in her seat to face him, pulled down her sleeves to better cover her fingers, and then took his warmer hand in hers again.

He placed his other hand over hers and rubbed, trying to keep the circulation moving. 'Because I do,' he said. 'I'm sure as soon as DCI Lake put the phone down, he would have made a call to Kirby Clark to see if he's really going to publish the story this morning.'

A shiver wormed its way down his spine. 'And when he hears that they are, he's going to have to wake up the Chief Constable and give him the news that they have to arrest the favourite candidate to run this country after next week's election.'

Erin leaned her head against her seat. 'I don't envy him that.'

'Me neither,' said Will. 'Either it's the best career move he's ever going to make, or he's finished.'

'He'll be fine.'

'Yes,' agreed Will. 'He will. He just won't realise it right at this moment.'

Erin looked out the passenger window into the dark woodland to the left of the car. 'I hope he's okay.'

Will squeezed her hand. 'Me too.'

She turned back to him. 'He really likes you, you know. I don't know – there's something about you. He doesn't often open up to people like he has to you. Or Amy.'

Will flexed his legs under the dashboard and flinched as his knee muscles threatened to cramp. 'That's why we have to do this,' he said eventually. 'I can't leave him there. I can't let Rossiter do this to him.'

He caught movement out the corner of his eye and turned his head as a pair of headlights flared in the distance and began barrelling along the main road.

'I think they're here.'

'What do we do?'

'Wait until they go past, then follow.'

'Will?' Erin's eyes were wide in the gloom of the car. 'Are they going to arrest us?'

'I don't know.'

His eyes opened wide as Erin snatched her fingers from his grasp, leaned across, and took his face between her hands.

'Thank you,' she whispered and kissed him.

Will closed his eyes, lost in the moment. Beyond the sensation of Erin's soft lips moving with his, he tried to recall when he'd been kissed so intensely, his heart racing.

Months? Years? When had he last really let go like this? Trusted someone with his life?

Erin pulled away as the police car flashed by, its siren silent, the blue and red beams from its emergency lights echoing off the trees that lined the road.

'Will?'

'I know.'

He reached down and turned the ignition key away from him, the engine powering to life. He was about to switch on the headlights when a second and then a third police car shot by, followed by an armed response vehicle, its navy panels silhouetted against the red and blue flash from the vehicles ahead of it.

'I think they took you seriously.' Erin watched the last of the vehicles shoot past them, then reached out and squeezed his hand. 'We should go.'

Will flicked the lights on, and pushed his foot on the throttle pedal, easing the car out of its hiding place and onto the lane. The brake lights of the armed response vehicle in front of them flickered once, and then disappeared as it turned the final corner in the road before the house.

His throat felt dry as he considered the implications of his decision to approach the police, wondering if DCI Lake and his superiors could be trusted. His thoughts turned to Mack and whether the old man knew they were coming, that he'd soon be free.

He couldn't – wouldn't – consider the fact that Erin's father might already be dead.

'Will!'

He slammed on the brakes as the car exited the corner.

The police vehicles were stationary at the side of the road, lights flashing. Silhouetted figures stood next to open car doors, and as Will edged the car forward, he realised the game was up.

He had to stop.

He indicated left and pulled behind the armed response vehicle, then wound down his window as a burly figure hurried towards the car, closely followed by two armed officers carrying MP5 submachine guns.

He blinked, then shielded his eyes with his hand and looked away as a flashlight shone across his face.

'Will Fletcher. Fancy seeing you here.' DCI Lake lowered the beam. 'Get out of the car. Who else is in there with you?'

'Erin Hogarth.'

'Out. Both of you. Now.'

Will turned, his gaze meeting Erin's. 'In case I don't get the chance to say this, thank you.'

She nodded, her eyes bright. She wiped at them with her sleeve, then reached out and pulled him closer.

'No, thank you,' she said and kissed him.

'Now!' barked the police officer.

Will pulled away from Erin and opened his door, placing his hand on the roof of the vehicle to steady himself, his legs shaking.

Lake waited until Erin had joined them, then glared at Will. 'What the hell are you doing here?'

'My father's being held by Ian Rossiter,' said Erin. 'He's been tortured.'

The policeman's gaze flicked from Erin to Will. 'Is that true?'

Will nodded. 'We got a phone call from Rossiter. Mack – Erin's dad – was screaming in the background.' He held out his mobile phone and replayed the voicemail message on speaker.

The detective paled, and then motioned to one of the junior constables standing on the periphery of the group, his eyes wide.

'Constable – an evidence bag please.'

Lake shook out the plastic bag and held it open to Will. 'Put your phone in there.'

Will did as he was instructed. 'Why?'

'It'll be used as evidence in the case,' said the detective. 'If this ever gets to court…' he added under his breath.

He turned to one of the armed officers next to him. 'Brief your men. Make any changes to your plan you need to, but we're going in in two minutes.'

The man nodded and ran back to the group of men standing by the vehicles watching the exchange, his colleague at his heels.

Lake waited until they were out of earshot then turned back to Will and Erin.

'You're coming with me.' He held up his hand. 'You're staying in the car with my driver. I'm not having you running around while we've got a potential armed suspect, or the future leader of this country under suspicion of murder. If you as much as open a window to get some fresh air, I'll have you both arrested, understand?'

They both nodded.

The detective pointed to his car. 'Get in.'

Chapter 40

Will rubbed his sleeve on the fogged-up window of the vehicle and peered through the glass.

Next to him, Erin stared at the back of Lake's head, her features calm, although Will knew she was as worried as he was, by the way her fingers clutched at his, entwined on the seat between them.

The driver leaned forward and adjusted the volume as the police radio crackled to life, then turned to the detective next to him.

'Confirmation received that Mr Rossiter is at home, sir.'

'Good.' Lake raised his mobile phone to his ear. 'We have a positive identification, team. Both cars are to follow mine. Car three – when we reach the house, you drive round to the back and stop anyone from leaving that way. Car two – you'll be entering the house with me. Drivers to stay with their vehicles, engines running at all times, is that understood?'

Will bit his lip and thought of Kirby putting the final touches to the front-page news article.

Whichever way Ian Rossiter chose to run, his life as a politician was over.

As the sun crested the horizon, Lake nodded, and the vehicle lurched forwards into the road. The driver manipulated the steering wheel with an efficiency that startled Will.

After half a mile, the car swept up to the gates of the house and slid to a halt on the loose gravel.

The driver lowered the window and pressed the security intercom.

It fizzled once, before the static gave way to a male voice.

'Rossiter,' hissed Erin.

Lake held his hand up and nodded to the driver.

'Good morning,' he said. 'This is Detective Chief Inspector Trevor Lake of the Metropolitan Police. Kindly open the gate, please. We have an urgent matter to discuss with you, Mr Rossiter.'

The occupants of the car held their breath as the silence stretched on before the voice returned.

'Proceed up to the house, please.'

A click ended the call, and then the gates began to swing inwards.

The detective raised the mobile phone to his lips. 'Now.'

The two police cars that had been following at a distance suddenly raced into view, placing themselves in a convoy behind the lead vehicle.

Will hung onto the armrest of the door as the driver floored the accelerator, sending up a spray of gravel under the wheels.

The three cars sped up the winding driveway towards the house, branching off as they approached into their agreed positions.

As the car stopped, Lake turned to Will and Erin.

'No matter what happens, you stay here, is that understood?'

Will nodded mutely and squeezed Erin's hand.

She opened her mouth to speak, but a glare from the police officer silenced her.

'You're here to identify Mackenzie Harris. Nothing else,' he added. 'If you leave this vehicle, my colleague here will arrest you – clear?'

'Yes.' Will nodded.

Erin sighed. 'Yes, okay.'

The detective climbed from the vehicle, signalled to his men, and began to walk towards the house.

Will watched as he approached the front door.

He stepped back as the door opened before he'd had a chance to knock, and Ian Rossiter glared out at the police officer on his doorstep.

Will wound down his window, ignoring the glare from the police driver, the men's voices faint, but audible.

'What do you want?' asked the politician, his voice carrying across the driveway, full of pomposity. 'What on earth could be so important that you have to disturb a man at this time of the morning?'

His face betrayed no sign of stress, and instead, he stood with his hands on his hips, his hair slightly ruffled as if he'd only just awoken. He wore beige trousers and a navy polo shirt, and Will noticed the shirt was untucked, giving the impression the man had dressed in a rush.

Rossiter frowned as three police officers climbed from the second car and began to walk up the path towards the house.

'What's going on?' he demanded.

'Mr Rossiter, this is a warrant to search your house,' said Lake and handed the paperwork over. 'We have reason to believe that one Mackenzie Harris is being held here against his will.'

'This is preposterous!' shouted Rossiter. 'I'll have your bloody career for this!'

His gaze turned to the vehicles at that moment and his jaw dropped. 'That little conniving bitch,' he said and looked at the police officer. 'Is she the one that's told you this? You know she's a pathological liar?'

His lip curled as he stared at Erin, and Will felt her tremble under his touch.

'It's okay,' he whispered. 'He can't get you here.'

He heard her swallow. 'He still terrifies me, Will,' she croaked. 'None of you know how dangerous he can be.'

She leaned forward to the driver. 'They're armed, aren't they?'

He gave an almost imperceptible nod. 'We took Mr Fletcher's story seriously, Miss Hogarth, don't worry.'

She fell back into her seat, and Will pulled her close. 'Not long now,' he murmured. 'Hang in there.'

He turned his attention back to the house.

'If you could move aside, sir,' said Lake. 'We'll make a start. Is there anyone else on the property with you?'

Rossiter's jaw bobbed up and down before he regained his composure. He seemed to take a deep breath before speaking. 'My press secretary Malcolm Gregory. Two friends that stayed last night – we were drinking quite late. Didn't seem worth the risk for them to drive home, so I invited them to stay.'

He smiled, and Will shuddered at how quickly the man could turn on the charm.

'Right, well if you could please ask your guests to join us, that would be appreciated,' said Lake. 'Shall we come in?'

Will watched as the police officer led the way into the house, the last man through placing an umbrella stand against the front door to keep it open.

The driver drummed his fingers on the steering wheel as all three of them stared at the gaping maw of the entranceway to the house, wondering what was going on inside.

'What happens if something goes wrong?' asked Erin. 'Have you thought of that?'

The driver glanced in the rear-view mirror and caught Will staring at him. 'There are two more cars back at the lay-by now,' he said. 'And an ambulance.'

Will's heart jumped between his ribs. If the police had already organised an ambulance, it meant they were taking the story seriously.

It also meant they were having serious doubts about Mack's survival.

Chapter 41

Gregory fed the papers into the fireplace and watched as the greedy flames devoured the documents, the edges curling and turning brown before disintegrating in the heat.

Beyond the room, he could hear Rossiter getting closer, the police no doubt at his heels, trying to hurry him along.

He cursed under his breath as a page fell from his fingers, bent down to pick it up and glanced at the numbers across the paper.

All their work. All this time.

'Shit,' he mumbled, screwing up the page in his hand and tossing it onto the fire.

He peered over his shoulder as the footsteps drew nearer, then turned and dropped the stack of documents into the grate and stirred them with the poker.

He glared at the hearth. The problem with old stately homes was that the chimneys were never swept as often as they should be. The draw wasn't enough to fan the flames, and smoke began to billow out into the room.

He coughed and moved back to his desk as the door opened.

'What's the meaning of this interruption?' he demanded as Rossiter stood to one side to let the police detective and his colleague over the threshold. His mind worked as he spoke. Two armed special response officers stood in the hallway outside. No doubt, the detective had more men posted by the front door and around the building. He congratulated himself at having the foresight to light the fire as soon as Rossiter had hammered on his office door and announced the police were about to descend on them.

He glanced towards the hearth, the smoke increasing in density, then back at the detective.

It was too late. The man had followed his gaze and now moved across the room to the grate.

Gregory watched as Lake crouched and began to pull pages from the flames, salvaging as much as possible. Soot and ash covered the hearthrug.

'Hey,' exclaimed Rossiter, 'that's original nineteenth century – you can't do that!'

'I can, sir,' said the detective. 'And I will. Destroying evidence is a crime.' He looked over his shoulder, his eyes finding Gregory. 'As I'm sure you're both aware.'

Gregory recovered quickly. 'As I'm sure you're aware, Detective, accusing a parliamentary candidate of a crime is extremely serious,' he said, coughing to clear the acrid smoke from his throat. He moved towards the window and released the safety catch before shoving the sash frame upwards, allowing fresh air into the room.

'No!'

Lake realised too late what was happening.

As the morning breeze seeped through the gap, the flames caught in the hearth, freshly fuelled by the fresh air filling the space. The remaining documents began to burn quickly, easily.

One of the other police officers joined the detective, and between them, they tried to pull more evidence from the flames.

Gregory glanced over at Rossiter, who gave an almost imperceptible nod. He didn't feel so confident as his boss. Many of the more important accounts were now lying, singed, on the floor in front of him.

He wiped a trace of sweat from his top lip with a handkerchief and looked away.

Lake cursed and eased himself upwards from his crouched position, then glared at Gregory. 'Gather what we have, constable. Take it out to one of the cars and tell the driver not to let the documents out of his sight.'

Once the constable had left the room, the detective turned back to Rossiter. 'Sir, we've reason to believe that there may be other people here. Perhaps not of their own volition?' He cocked an eyebrow.

Rossiter shrugged and said nothing.

'What's going on?' said Gregory, stalling them for as long as possible. 'What on earth are you doing here, forcing yourselves into Mr Rossiter's private residence?'

'We didn't force ourselves,' said Lake. 'Mr Rossiter here answered the front door and invited us in.' He turned to the politician, who nodded.

Gregory cursed under his breath. 'Then you won't mind if I call our legal representatives,' he said.

'You can, once I ascertain that no one is being held in this building against their will,' replied the detective. He turned, ignoring Gregory, and spoke to Rossiter. 'If you wouldn't mind giving us the guided tour, sir.'

He gestured towards the door.

'I'll join you,' said Gregory, moving from behind his desk. The last thing he wanted was Rossiter opening his mouth and making a disastrous situation worse for both of them. Already his mind was working quickly, trying to fathom how on earth he was going to extricate himself from the situation and create a modicum of distance between him and his employer.

***

Gregory's fears were realised as he trooped after Rossiter and the police officers towards the back of the house.

The man cheerily pointed out antiques, extolling the history of the building as he strolled ahead of them, seemingly oblivious to the seriousness of the situation.

Rossiter had been acting strange ever since they'd finished torturing the old man, and Gregory suspected that his boss had taken even more of the strong painkillers he was quickly becoming addicted to.

What's he doing?

He became more concerned as he followed the small group through to the back of the house, and then his heart lurched.

Rossiter was headed straight for the kitchen instead of taking the police round to the other side of the house as they'd agreed before the detective had knocked on the front door. Which meant their security team wouldn't have had time to remove the Irishman from the premises.

He stumbled forward. 'No!'

Rossiter flung open the door, stood to one side, and ushered the police into the room.

Gregory ran a hand over his face as he leaned against the doorframe and wondered what was going through the senior police detective's mind as he surveyed the gloomy space.

Mackenzie Harris sat in a chair in the middle of the room, his face bruised and bloody. His hands were folded in his lap and he peered up at the detective through puffy eyelids. One eye was red and weeping.

Two men in jeans and black sweaters stood with their backs to the wall opposite, the taller of the two with a knife still in his hands, both of them with their jaws open in shock.

Remnants of rope lay scattered on the floor around Mack's feet, and he rubbed at his wrists as he blinked and stared up at the newcomers.

'I never thought I'd say it, but I'm glad to see the police,' he said, then turned his head and spat on the floor, blood mixing with his saliva. 'What kept you?'

Lake turned to face Rossiter. 'You'd better explain yourself, Mr Rossiter – or should I address you as Terry Hollister?'

The politician baulked at the use of his real name, and then pointed at Mack. 'This man was caught trying to break into my house,' he said. 'My security people took the appropriate action.'

Gregory closed his eyes. *We're dead men.*

'Appropriate action?' the detective said. 'Explain to me how you consider this,' he waved his hand in Mack's direction, 'appropriate action?'

Rossiter smiled and moved to the butcher's block in the middle of the room. 'He was carrying this,' he said and turned.

Gregory's ears filled with the noise of three armed response policeman simultaneously raising their weapons and aiming them at Rossiter, who held up a revolver, its grey surface catching the sunlight beginning to pour through the kitchen window. He turned it in his hands, a wild look in his eyes.

'Put the gun down, sir,' said the detective, his voice strained. 'Right now.'

'But don't you see?' said Rossiter. 'He came here to kill me. We had to stop him.'

'Sir, put the gun down.'

'Ian, please,' begged Gregory. 'This has gone too far. Do what he says.'

Rossiter's eyes met his, before he swung the gun and rested the barrel under his chin.

'Sorry, Malcolm.'

'No!' yelled Lake.

Gregory flinched as the gun went off and closed his eyes.

A shocked silence filled the room, and then everyone began to talk at once.

Lake began barking orders, the tactical team aimed their weapons at Gregory's two security men, shouting at them to kneel on the floor with their hands raised.

The other officers began to clear out of the room, talking into their radios, their faces pale but their actions efficient and precise.

Gregory leaned against the wall, his legs shaking, his mouth open, and his mind still trying to process what he was staring at.

He's gone.

Rossiter's body had collapsed to the floor, blood pooling from the gaping wound in his skull.

Red and white spatter covered the stainless steel front of the oven and marble bench top, dripping down the cabinet doors to the floor next to the body.

Most of Rossiter's face had disintegrated under the force of the blast, and Gregory turned away, sickened.

He became aware of movement from the other side of the room and watched, horrified, as Mack staggered forward.

He leaned over and spat at Rossiter, his spittle landing on the dead man's feet. 'Good fucking riddance.'

Gregory's head jerked towards the Irishman, a moment before he launched himself across the kitchen at him.

'You bastard – you ruined everything!' he screamed.

Two policemen moved in front of him, their bulk blocking his way, forcing him to a standstill, before one of them unhooked handcuffs from his utility belt and slipped them over the press secretary's wrists.

Terror filled Gregory's veins. Without Rossiter to protect him, his chances of surviving prison were slim.

He shook off the constable's grip on his shoulder, his upper lip curling. 'Get your hands off me.' He pivoted until he faced Lake. 'I'll have your career for this,' he snarled.

'I doubt it,' said Lake. 'I've just lost one suspect. I have no intention of losing you.' He stepped closer. 'Malcolm Gregory, also known as Peter Hardcastle, I'm arresting you under suspicion of holding a man against his will and torture. You'll also be asked to provide a statement explaining your involvement in the fatal shooting of Amy Peters, Mr Rossiter's driver, and his bodyguard on Monday.'

The detective turned to one of the constables standing next to him. 'Take him away,' he said, before looking at Mack.

'You're coming with us, too.'

Chapter 42

Will's eyelids flew open at the sound of a loud *crack* from the house, closely followed by shouting.

Erin pushed herself away from him, and they both leaped from their seats and opened the car doors.

'Stay where you are!' hollered the police driver.

He got out of the vehicle and ran over to Erin who was racing towards the house. He pulled her into a vice-like grip and marched her back to the car, ignoring her struggles.

Pushing her towards Will, he pulled out a gun from a holster under his jacket. 'Keep hold of her. Get behind the car and *stay down.*'

He nodded to the other driver, who was leaning out of his car window, a worried expression on his face, and then pressed a button on his mobile phone.

'Team leader to back up team. Get here now. And bring that damn ambulance with you!'

He ended the call and dropped into a firing position, aiming at the front door of the house.

Will pulled Erin with him and fell to the ground behind the car. He hugged Erin closer to him, the metalwork of the vehicle pressing into his spine, his knees grazed by the gravel beneath them.

He stretched his neck and turned his head until he was level with the car window and peered through the glass.

Beyond the vehicle, the two police drivers were crouched, weapons ready.

He looked over his shoulder at the sound of engines revving over the crunch of gravel, then watched as two more police cars slid to a halt and their occupants spilled out onto the driveway. An ambulance braked, parking behind them, the faces of the two emergency workers grim as they stared through the windscreen.

He spun round at a shout from the front of the house and felt Erin move beside him.

Lake appeared, gun raised in the air. 'It's okay, lads. Stand down.'

The two policemen lowered their weapons and stood, brushing dirt off their uniforms.

Lake looked over his shoulder, and then turned, before reappearing with Mack.

Erin cried out in relief and collapsed against Will, whose own legs almost gave way.

'Thank god,' he murmured. 'I thought we'd lost him.'

As the two men drew closer, Will noticed the purple bruises covering Mack's face. One eye was so swollen, only a slit remained. He frowned, noticing how Lake kept a firm grip on Mack's arm on the way to the car.

When they were nearly level with the car, the police officer released the older man.

'You've got five minutes,' he said and went to stand over by the vehicle.

Will frowned as Mack approached on unsteady legs. The man's clothes were stained with dirt, but something else too.

A smile was plastered across the old man's face, and when he'd passed the police driver, his good eye winked at Will.

He grasped Erin's hands when he reached her.

'He won't be causing you any more harm, lass,' he said. 'I made sure of that.'

A sob escaped Erin's lips, and Mack released her hands.

Will pulled her to him, watching Mack over her head while he soothed her hair.

'What did you do?'

Mack stiffened, and his whole body grew taller. 'I did what needed to be done,' he said.

Will blinked, and then glanced up as Lake approached.

'Time's up, Mackenzie,' he said. 'Let's go. I have a feeling you and I are in for a long day.'

***

Will nodded his thanks at the junior constable who handed a coffee to him before leaving the waiting room. He wrapped his fingers around the smooth plastic surface, closed his eyes, and inhaled the aroma, his nose wrinkling.

'Don't get too excited. That one even manages to burn the instant stuff,' growled Lake.

Will opened his eyes. 'They say it's the thought that counts.'

'Huh.' Lake caught the attention of the desk sergeant. 'Derek – I'll take interview room three – can you mark it on the system for me?'

'Sir.'

The detective turned his attention back to Will. 'Follow me.'

He led the way down the corridor, into the heart of the police station. Will's ears roared with the force of his heart beating, adrenalin still soaring through his veins.

The backpack seemed heavy on his shoulder now, something he hadn't noticed before, and he ached to be rid of the fear that had consumed him for the past five days.

Five days. Was that all?

The detective paused at a closed door, used his security swipe card to open it, and then stood aside to let Will pass.

'Have a seat.' He gestured to the table in the centre of the room, four chairs surrounding it.

On the desk, a recording machine had been set up alongside a manila folder and two plastic evidence bags.

Will worked his way round until he could face the door and pulled out one of the chairs. As he sat, he noticed the loops on the edge of the table for handcuffs to be fixed to, if required.

The senior police officer joined him, hit the 'record' button on the machine, and then pushed a newspaper across the table to Will, the front page facing upwards, its bold headline and accompanying photograph already imprinted on Will's memory.

'I presume this was your way of having some insurance?'

Will nodded. 'I wasn't sure you'd believe me. Or if I could trust you.'

The policeman shrugged himself back into his seat and checked his watch before he paused to clear his throat and looked down at his notes.

'All right,' he said. 'You've told me the version the newspaper's going to print. What don't they know?'

'What do you mean?'

The detective folded his arms across his chest. 'Come on, Will. You don't expect me to believe that Amy *just happened* to stumble on this story, do you? And that your own *father* somehow provided the missing evidence some twenty years after he went missing?' He leaned forwards. 'The truth, Will. Now.'

'I don't know what you mean.'

'Really? Let me show you.'

The detective moved round the table, glared at Will, then bent down and picked up his backpack.

Will rubbed his palms over his jeans as he watched the policeman unzip the bag and pull out an object.

Lake dropped the bag to the floor and set the object on the table.

Will's hands moved towards the robot toy before he could stop.

'Do you know what I think Will? I think you've engineered this from the start.' The detective sat in his chair and folded his hands on the table, his eyes boring into Will's. He pointed at the toy. 'This has all been about revenge, hasn't it? But not just for Amy.

This has always been about what happened to your father, hasn't it?'

Will bit his lip, his fingers moving the parts of the toy as Lake spoke, turning it from a robot into a car. He set it flat on the table and began to run it backwards and forwards, the tiny plastic tyres gripping the surface.

'It took me weeks to fix this,' he said. 'There were so many missing parts. I wouldn't let my mum vacuum for days. Not until I was sure I had them all.'

'Will? How did you find Rossiter in the first place? You used Amy, didn't you?'

'One of the neighbours helped me,' Will said, turning the car and pulling it back towards him. 'Mum wouldn't let me use the glue on my own. She was scared I'd hurt myself.'

His fingers began to twist the parts once more, turning it back into a robot.

'Will!'

He jumped as the detective's hand slapped the table and raised his eyes.

'How the hell did you trick Amy into helping you?' he said. 'What happened? Did you latch onto her at university? Realise she was an asset?' He stood and began to pace the room. 'Did you even stop to think of the danger you'd be putting her in? Just to expose Rossiter the way you did? For Christ's sake, Will! She was your girlfriend – or didn't that mean anything to you?'

'She wasn't my girlfriend.'

'What?' Lake stopped pacing. 'What did you say?'

Will sighed. 'She wasn't my girlfriend.'

'Since when? She gets shot, ends up in a coma, and dies – and you decide to move on and sleep with Erin, is that the way this goes?'

'No. She wasn't my girlfriend.' Will stared at the detective, his arms crossed.

The man moved closer and leaned on the table. 'Then who the hell was she, Will?'

'My sister.'

Chapter 43

Belfast, Northern Ireland – Autumn 1999

Everyone turned at a surprised shout from the hallway.

The boy's sister suddenly appeared from the living room where she'd been hiding, raced into the kitchen, and levelled a kick at the leader's head as he bent down to strike her father once more.

The gangster roared in pain, rose from his crouching position, and launched across the room at the girl, where she'd retreated to a corner next to the pantry.

Grabbing her by the arm, he pushed her hard, towards her mother.

Except that the force of his anger carried her momentum past the arms of her mother.

Instead, the little girl stumbled, lost her balance, and fell against the edge of the kitchen table.

She crumpled into a heap on the floor, where she lay unmoving.

A deadly silence filled the room before the boy's mother began to wail as she crawled across the floor to her daughter.

'Oh my god, what have you done? What have you done?' the boy's father cried. He began to raise himself up off the floor, wiping blood from his nose and mouth as he tried to steady his rocking body.

The leader crossed the floor in a heartbeat and planted his boot in the small of the man's back, forcing him to the ground once more.

'Stay still, you bastard. We haven't finished with you yet.'

The boy's eyes widened as his mother reached his sister and gathered the girl's motionless body to her. As she gently turned the girl's face, the boy noticed the deep cut to the girl's forehead, an angry red line that started at her eyebrow and tapered towards her hairline.

'My baby, my poor baby,' his mother wailed.

The girl's eyes remained closed, her face immobile and devoid of expression. To the boy, she appeared to be sleeping.

'Is she breathing?' asked his father, his voice muffled through broken teeth. 'Can you feel a heartbeat?'

'What the fuck is going on?' The younger intruder's voice floated from the front door. 'What's happening?'

'Shut up. Just stay where you are.' The shorter of the three intruders turned his attention back to the boy's mother and sister.

He bent down next to the mother and prised away her hands. 'Let me see.'

The woman slapped his hands away. 'Stay away from her, you bastard. Don't you touch my baby.'

He hit her face, the sound reverberating around the kitchen.

She rocked back on her feet in shock, and he took that moment to pluck the unconscious girl from her lap.

The boy watched, stunned, as the man ripped open the collar of the little girl's jumper and placed his fingers against her neck.

'Still a pulse,' he grunted. 'She's just out cold.'

'She needs an ambulance!' begged the boy's father. 'For pity's sake – let us call an ambulance for her!'

He cried out in pain as the leader's boot turned against his skin.

'We're not calling an ambulance,' the man hissed. 'Not until we've finished with you.'

He bent down and hauled the boy's father to his feet. 'Now, where have you hidden the photograph, eh? Where do we find it?'

The boy's father staggered, his head lolling to one side. 'I have no idea what you're talking about,' he whispered.

'So be it,' said the gangster. He removed a gun from his waistband and slammed the butt of it across the man's cheek bone, then aimed a punch at the man's stomach.

The small boy glared at the masked man, his fists clenched, and rushed at the gangster's leader.

'Leave my dad alone!' Will collided with the back of his legs and pushed him off balance.

The man grunted in surprise, and the boy's father stepped forward, knocking his arm upwards.

The sound of gunfire exploded in the small space.

Will's mother screamed, while the shorter of the three thugs rushed to help his accomplice.

'Are you shot? Did the bastard shoot you?'

The leader shoved him away and swung round to face the boy's father who was backed against the kitchen sink, panting, his eyes wide.

Will watched as both men glanced at the ceiling, a small hole raining plaster dust onto the kitchen tiles between them.

Then the leader swung the gun across his father's face once more.

Blood sprayed across the kitchen cabinet and he cried out, clutching his mouth and nose.

The thug then swept round to face Will and backhanded him across his cheek before shoving him hard.

Will stumbled, and cried out as his backside hit the kitchen floor, the shock jarring his hips.

'Please, stop it – don't hurt them!' cried his mother. 'Whatever it is you want, please – just take it, then go!'

'Boss, we're out of time – the neighbours will have heard the shot,' murmured the shorter man. 'We'll have to take him with us.'

The leader tucked his gun back into the waistband of his jeans, then grabbed the boy's father roughly and spun him round to face the back door. 'Move.'

He turned and shouted over his shoulder to the youngest of the three, still standing at the front door. 'We're leaving – come on.'

'No!'

'Billy – go back inside!' urged his father as he was dragged down the garden towards the back gate. 'Look after your sister – get help for her!'

His words were faint under the torrential rain, a cold wind howling through the back yards of the terraced houses, sending debris flying in the air.

'Daddy!'

'I love you, Billy...'

His words were cut short as the leader punched him in the stomach and he collapsed onto the grass, gasping.

The men opened the back gate and then returned for the boy's father, dragging him from the ground and balancing his weight between them.

'Go, go!' urged the leader. 'Down the alleyway – he's waiting at the car for us!'

'Daddy!' screamed Will and stepped from the warmth of the kitchen. 'No!'

He began to run after the men who were pushing his father through the gate, but then stopped as the leader spun on his heel and aimed the gun at him.

'Stay there, boy, or I swear to God I'll put a bullet through your skull.'

Will slid to the ground, and then whimpered as urine trickled down his legs.

The man nodded. 'That's right, boy. Stay where you are.' He turned and ran after his accomplices.

Will began to sob, huge choking cries that wracked his small frame. He tumbled from the back step and crossed the wet grass, his hair and clothing soaked in seconds.

He ignored the cold seeping through his socks and hurried to the back gate. He slowed as he approached, then stopped and peered round the frame.

Four shadowy figures, one stumbling between the arms of two others, reached the end of the alleyway, their silhouettes muted by the rain-filled pyramids of street lighting.

A car skidded to a stop in front of them, and the boy watched as his father was shoved into the back seat, and the three attackers jumped into the vehicle before it sped away.

It was only then that Will's attention was drawn back to the house, and the sound of his mother's wailing.

He ran back to the open kitchen door and stepped inside, water pooling around his feet.

His mother sat on the floor, his sister cradled in her arms. Blood pooled from the cut above the small girl's eyebrow, and she lay still, as if asleep.

His head twitched round as a pounding began on the front door, shouts beyond from the neighbours trying to enter.

'Get them, Billy – let them in!' urged his mother. 'Tell them to call an ambulance!'

Will raced from the room and down the hallway. He swallowed as he reached for the latch and regret consumed him.

If only he hadn't opened the door. If only he'd been braver and attacked the masked man sooner. If only...

Mr Matthews from next door stood on the front step, his face ashen. 'Billy – what on earth's happened?'

Behind him, four other men, also neighbours, peered over his shoulder. One carried a baseball bat.

As the shock of the past few minutes taking over his emotions, Will's bottom lip trembled. He pointed towards the kitchen and stepped back as the men pushed by and went to his mother's aid.

As the voices from the kitchen washed over him, Will slumped to the floor in the hallway, the front door still open, his robot toy abandoned, forgotten.

In the distance, a siren began to wail, and he let the tears streak down his face as the emergency services drew closer.

Chapter 44

Will unfolded his arms and leaned on the table as the detective pulled out his chair and ran his hand over his face.

'Keep talking.'

'After dad was taken, our mum fell to pieces. Sure, the neighbours helped where they could, but I got into trouble at school – truancy, that sort of thing. About a year later, one of mum's cousins turned up and took us all back to England to live with her. In a way, it was good – it got mum the care she needed.'

'But?'

'It felt like they were trying to forget dad,' said Will. 'It was like they were trying to pretend it didn't happen.'

'Maybe they were scared?'

Will snorted. 'Of course they were.' He ran a hand through his hair. 'It was pretty obvious that the police were never going to find out what happened to my dad, so when I was about fifteen, I mentioned to Amy that perhaps we should try.' He smiled. 'She was really into her mystery books and already talking about going to university, so I encouraged her. Suggested she look at becoming a journalist.' He leaned back in his chair. 'She was a natural.'

'So you waited until she got out of university, then turned her loose, is that it?'

'Pretty much.'

'What did you do in the meantime?'

'Kept my head down and my eyes and ears open. We had scraps of information – things we'd overheard as kids, stuff the police would tell mum when they phoned with updates. Amy started researching archived newspaper articles about organised crime in Northern Ireland back when the peace accord negotiations were taking place – Belfast was rife with armed gangs. Some of the names sounded familiar, so we started there and she began to establish a pattern.'

'Which is how she traced Mack.'

'I guess.'

Lake took a sip of water, and then turned the glass in his hand. 'What I don't understand, Will, is if she had all this information, why didn't she tell you? Why send you cryptic messages and send you running round half the country to piece this together once she'd been shot? What went wrong?'

Will looked down at his hands. 'We had a disagreement on Sunday night.'

'What sort of disagreement?'

Will sighed. 'It was stupid, just one of those stupid arguments that happen.'

'Go on.'

'She wouldn't tell me what she'd found out because she was scared what I would do with that information.' He picked up the robot toy and turned it in his hand. 'She was worried that I'd kill whoever killed our dad.'

Lake leaned back in his chair and stared at Will. 'And would you?'

'At the time, I was pretty angry, yeah.' He paused. 'But in hindsight, what Amy proposed made a lot more sense. I was going to tell her Monday morning that she was right, that I'd do what she said.'

He wiped his eyes. 'She was a great reporter. It would have made her a star.' He sniffled. 'But when I went to apologise, she'd already gone. I didn't get the chance,' he whispered.

The detective moved across the room, picked up a box of tissues from a corner cabinet, and slid it across the table to Will.

'I'm not even going to bother trying to tell you that you should've brought everything you had to us,' he said.

Will nodded, pulled a tissue from the box, and blew his nose. 'I know we should have,' he said. 'But trust me when you've spent most of your life listening to people tell you they can't help, that they can't do anything for you, you give up – or fix it yourself.'

'Did you know Mack was going to go to Rossiter's house?'

Will shook his head. 'I thought Rossiter's men found Mack and took him there.'

'So you've never seen this?'

Will's eyes opened wide as the detective pushed a plastic bag across the table towards him. Inside, a revolver shone under the plastic, despite the white forensic powder that blotched its surface in places.

'No,' he said. 'Should I have?'

The policeman's lips pursed and he pushed a second plastic wallet across the desk.

Will recognised the photograph. It was the one Mack had given to him, the one he'd handed over to the detective on their arrival at the police station.

The one his dad had taken.

He blinked, not understanding.

'It's the same gun, Will.'

He glanced across at the detective, then reached out, picked up the plastic wallet, and squinted at the image.

'Are you sure?'

'I'm sure.' Lake leaned back in his chair. 'In fact, as we speak, my colleagues are talking with our counterparts in Northern Ireland about a cold case they have. A businessman who turned up dead several years ago, a single gunshot wound to his head.'

He leaned forward and tapped the photograph, then the gun.

'I'm not usually a betting man, Mr Fletcher, but I'll wager the ballistics match this gun.'

Will sensed the pieces falling into place. 'Mack never meant to shoot Rossiter, did he?' he said in wonder.

The detective shook his head. 'I don't believe so, no. I think he wanted to make sure that gun was in Rossiter's possession when we turned up.' The policeman gathered the evidence bags together. 'I don't think even he imagined that Rossiter would take his own life.'

'Mack didn't shoot him?'

'No. Rossiter panicked,' said Lake. 'Caught us all by surprise. The moment he realised he was going to be placed under arrest, he shot himself.'

Will exhaled, a wave of relief engulfing him. 'So Mack's free to leave?'

'I'm afraid not,' said the detective. He folded his arms on the table. 'Mack's been a wanted man for years, Will. He's not innocent. He did some pretty bad things in his time.'

Will opened his mouth to ask what Mack had done, then thought better of it. 'What will happen to him?'

'He's been formally charged.' Lake rubbed a hand across his eyes, and Will realised for the first time how exhausted the policeman looked. 'Given his past track record, he's going to be looking at a long sentence.'

'You know he has cancer?'

Lake nodded. 'And he'll get looked after by the prison authorities; don't worry. In fact,' he sighed. 'He'll probably last longer in prison than he would have in that damp two-up two-down he was renting.' He leaned forward. 'Is there anything else you need to tell me, Will?'

Will shook his head.

'I need you to state that out loud,' said Lake, pointing at the recorder.

'No,' said Will. 'There's nothing else. That's it.' He reached for another tissue and wiped his eyes, drained of all emotion.

The detective stopped the voice recorder, stood, and motioned Will towards the door. 'One of our people will be in touch once this has been typed up,' he said. 'You're welcome to go and wait in the cafeteria on the second floor – there's a television there and magazines. You'll be asked to read through the statement and sign it.'

'And Erin?'

'She's been speaking to a female police officer. We have her statement as well.' He led Will along the corridor. 'Come on, I'll show you where you can wait.'

Will followed him towards the elevators, their footsteps muted on the faded blue carpet.

As they turned the corner into the reception area, his gaze found Erin's, and she rose from her seat, her face pale.

He met her halfway, wrapped his arms around her, and buried his face in her hair.

'It's over,' he whispered.

She raised her eyes to his. 'Thank you.'

They moved towards the cafeteria, the senior policeman showing them where to find the coffee machine before leaving them alone with the instruction they were to stay in the room until he returned.

Will waited until Erin had sat, then fetched them a hot drink and switched on the small television in the corner.

Grabbing the remote control, he joined her at the table and sifted through the channels, surfing aimlessly between the programmes.

'Wait.' Erin's hand hovered over the remote. 'Go back.'

Will pressed the button until a news bulletin appeared, the familiar red and white logo next to the reporter's face, and turned up the volume.

'*Sources close to Mr Rossiter's political party are currently unavailable for comment regarding the allegations that appeared in the newspaper earlier this morning. However we understand that Mr Rossiter was wounded in a home invasion last night...*'

They both turned at the sound of footsteps to see the detective standing in the doorway.

'Home invasion?' said Will. 'Is that how this is going to be reported?'

'For the moment,' said Lake. 'In about an hour, the Chief Commissioner will make a statement, saying that we're looking into allegations of corruption.'

He joined them at the table. 'We have to work with the media and the government on this, Will.

We're going to tell the public the truth, but we have to manage the process.' He held up his hand. 'It's in your interests as well. The last thing we want is for you to be hounded by the press. And they will.' He glanced back to the screen. 'At least this way, you get the chance to make some alternative living arrangements.'

Will rubbed his eyes. 'They're going to be like a pack of wolves, aren't they?'

'Yes, they are.'

They turned at the sound of someone clearing his throat to see a junior constable standing in the doorway, a pen and a sheaf of papers in his hand.

The detective took the documents and dismissed him, then put the pages on the table, one set in front of Will and the other next to Erin.

'For you. Read it through. Make sure you're happy with it before signing.'

Will took his typed statement and sank onto one of the plastic chairs, his eyes skimming the words. He wiped away the tears that threatened to fall as he realised the pages signified an end to his life as he'd known it. All he'd ever wanted was revenge, and it scared him what he had lost in that pursuit, and that he didn't yet know how he was going to fill the gap.

Erin moved beside him, and then leaned her head on his shoulder. 'We'll be okay, Will.'

He slipped an arm around her and picked up the pen. He paused and glanced up to see the detective watching him, his arms crossed, his expression pensive. Will nodded, then began to scratch his signature at the foot of each page and handed the document over.

'Thank you.' Lake took the pages and slipped them into a folder. 'I'll show you the way out.'

Will took Erin's hand and pulled her to her feet. 'Come on. Let's go.'

They moved towards the elevators, and Will punched the button.

'What will you do when you leave here?' asked the detective, passing the paperwork to the desk sergeant and joining them.

Will shrugged. 'I'm not sure,' he mumbled.

He glanced up at the sound of a *ping* and pulled Erin to one side to let a young policewoman pass before they stepped into the empty elevator.

Lake held out his hand to stop the doors closing. 'If I could make a suggestion?'

Will lifted his head. 'What?'

'Leave it to the experts next time.'

Chapter 45

Will held his mother's hand as they stood at the graveside together, the sun's rays catching the leaves of the enormous oak trees above them, casting a dappled light onto the freshly mown grass at their feet.

The private ceremony had been short, attended only by Will, his mother, and Erin, but the words of the eulogy had been heartfelt and delivered with appropriate respect by the ageing vicar.

Flowers from Amy's colleagues at the newspaper covered the coffin, her editor respecting Will's mother's request for privacy to mourn.

His mother squeezed his hand, then bent down and picked up a handful of the freshly dug soil next to the graveside, closed her fingers, and kissed them before releasing the dirt onto the coffin below.

Will wiped at the tears that had begun to course down his cheeks, and then took the handkerchief Erin held out to him.

'Thanks,' he mumbled.

His voice shook, the finality of the moment hitting him like a punch to the stomach. He bent down and scooped up a handful of the soil, closed his fist around it, and kissed his fingers.

'Night, sis.'

He relaxed his grip and let the dirt fall from his hand, tears streaking his cheeks. A shuddering sigh left him as the last of the soil fell between his fingers, and he turned to his mother.

'Come here,' she said. 'Walk with me.'

He followed his mother along the gravel path, Erin several paces behind, giving them time alone.

One of the carers from the hospice waited next to a liveried four-door sedan, the logo of the care home splashed along its sides.

His mother stopped when they were several paces from the car, reached up and held his face between her hands, her eyes bright.

'Your dad would've been so proud of you, Will,' she said. 'And I am, too.'

'I lost Amy,' he whispered. 'It's my fault she's dead.'

'No!' His mother's response was emphatic. 'No, you're not responsible, Will. The man who was responsible is dead. Never forget that.' She patted his cheek gently, and then drew him into her arms. 'Amy chose to go after Rossiter without you. I'm proud of her, too. But you need to move on from this, Will. Your dad and Amy would have wanted that.'

'I don't think I know how to.'

She patted his cheek once more then began to walk towards the waiting car.

The carer took her arm and gently helped her into the vehicle. Before the door was closed, his mother's gaze flickered behind Will, to where Erin stood, and then back to him before she smiled.

'You'll work it out.'

As the car pulled away, Erin slipped her hand into his and squeezed.

'What are you going to do now?'

He shrugged. 'I don't know.'

'Can I make a suggestion?'

'Go on.'

She stopped, pulling him to a halt. 'Let it go now, Will. It's done.'

He pulled her into a hug and stared over the top of her head at the gravedigger and his assistant waiting patiently under one of the oak trees, a thin trail of blue smoke lifting into the air from their cigarettes.

'You're probably right,' he murmured, then took Erin's hand and led her back to the car.

'Revenge is an ugly master.'

THE END

From the Author

Thanks for purchasing and reading *Look Closer* – I hope you enjoyed it. A lot of people don't realise that the best way to help an author is to write a review – if you did enjoy this story, please leave a few words with the retailer you bought it from, or on one of the book review websites.

Don't forget to join my mailing list for exclusive offers and giveaways by completing the form on my website at: www.rachelamphlett.com

I look forward to hearing from you.

Printed in Great Britain
by Amazon